The Pods Are Alive and Well and . . .

The Doctor reached the top of the stairs. It was dark and dusty, and there was very little head room. Through the gloom he could just make out a door down a narrow passage. He clambered along and tried the knob. The door opened to reveal an attic with a second door that led onto the roof of the house. He crawled out. To his left was a large section made of glass. He edged toward it and peered through.

The sight that met him made his blood run cold. Twenty feet below in the room, Sarah was imprisoned in a chair with one arm clamped to a wooden bench. Less than twelve inches away lay the pod, hideously swollen and vibrating menacingly. Even as the Doctor looked it began to break open. . . .

The Fourth Doctor Who

This episode features the fourth Doctor Who, who has survived three incarnations. The long trailing scarf, the floppy wide-brimmed hat, the mop of curly hair and the wide-eyed stare—all these are the obvious trademarks of the fourth Doctor Who. Along with a delightful mix of personality traits: genius and clown, hero and buffoon—the fourth Doctor Who combines the best of all who preceded him.

Doctor Who's Companion

SARAH JANE SMITH

Sarah is an independent freelance journalist. She has a mind of her own and once, while in search of a story, stowed away on Doctor Who's TARDIS—and ended up in the medieval past. Forever swearing she will never again set foot in the TARDIS, Sarah cannot resist the Doctor's plea that she accompany him one more time. While Sarah appears quite invulnerable, she really does need a bit of protection now and then.

#10

DOCTOR WHO

AND THE SEEDS OF DOOM

Philip Hinchcliffe

PINNACLE BOOKS LOS ANGELES

This is a work of fiction. All the characters and events portrayed in this book are fictional, and any resemblance to real people or incidents is purely coincidental.

DOCTOR WHO #10:
DOCTOR WHO AND THE SEEDS OF DOOM

A Pinnacle Books edition, published by special arrangement with W. H. Allen & Co., Ltd.
First published in Great Britain.

First printing, March 1980

ISBN: 0-523-40639-8

Cover illustration by David Mann

Printed in the United States of America

PINNACLE BOOKS, INC.
2029 Century Park East
Los Angeles, California 90067

Contents

Introducing DOCTOR WHO

amenities performed by HARLAN ELLISON

They could not have been more offended, confused, enraged and startled. . . . There was a moment of stunned silence. . . . and then an eruption of angry voices from all over the fifteen-hundred-person audience. The kids in their Luke Skywalker pajamas (cobbled up from older brother's castoff karate *gi*) and the retarded adults spot-welded into their Darth Vader fright-masks howled with fury. But I stood my ground, there on the lecture platform at the World Science Fiction Convention, and I repeated the heretical words that had sent them into animal hysterics:

"*Star Wars* is adolescent nonsense; *Close Encounters* is obscurantist drivel; 'Star Trek' can turn your brains to purée of bat guano; and the greatest science fiction series of all time is *Doctor Who*! And I'll take you all on, one-by-one or all in a bunch to back it up!"

Auditorium monitors moved in, truncheons ready to club down anyone foolish enough to try jumping the lecture platform; and finally there was relative silence. And I heard scattered voices screaming from the back of the room, "Who?" And I said, "Yes. Who!"

(It was like that old Abbott and Costello routine: Who's on first? No, Who's on third; What's on first.)

After a while we got it all sorted out and they understood that when I said Who I didn't mean whom, I meant Who . . . Doctor Who . . . the most famous science fiction character on British television. The renegade Time Lord, the far traveler through Time and

Space, the sword of justice from the Planet Gallifrey, the scourge of villains and monsters the galaxy over. The one and only, the incomparable, the bemusing and bewildering Doctor Who, the humanistic defender of Good and Truth whose exploits put to shame those of Kimball Kinnison, Captain Future and pantywaist nerds like Han Solo and Luke Skywalker.

My hero! Doctor Who!

For the American reading (and television-viewing) audience (and in this sole, isolated case I hope they're one and the same) Doctor Who is a new factor in the equation of fantastic literature. Since 1963 the Doctor and his exploits have been a consistent element of British culture. But we're only now being treated to the wonderful universes of Who here in the States. For those of us who were exposed to both the TV series on BBC and the long series of Doctor Who novels published in Great Britain, the time of solitary proselytizing is at an end. All we need to do now is thrust a Who novel into the hands of the unknowledgeable, or drag the unwary to a TV set and turn it on as the good Doctor goes through his paces. That's all it takes. Try this book and you'll understand.

I envy you your first exposure to this amazing conceit. And I wish for you the same delight I felt when Michael Moorcock, the finest fantasist in the English-speaking world, sat me down in front of his set in London, turned on the telly, and said, "Now be quiet and just watch."

That was in 1975. And I've been hooked on Doctor Who ever since. Understand: I despise television (having written it for sixteen years) and I spend much of my time urging people to bash in their picture tubes with Louisville Sluggers, to free themselves of the monster of the coaxial cable. And so, you must perceive that I speak of something utterly extraordinary and marvelous when I suggest you watch the Doctor Who series in whatever syndicated slot your local station has scheduled it. You must recognize that I risk all credibility for future exhortations by telling you *this* TV viewing will not harm you . . . will, in fact, delight and uplift you, stretch your imagination, tickle your risibilities, flinch your intellect of all lesser visual sf affections, improve your disposition and clean up your zits. What I'm saying here, in case you're a *yotz* who needs things codified simply and directly, is that "Doctor Who" is the apex, the pinnacle, the tops, the Louvre Museum, the tops, the Coliseum, and other etcetera.

Now to give you a few basic facts about the Doctor, to brighten your path through this nifty series of lunatic novels.

He is a Time Lord: one of that immensely wise and powerful super-race of alien beings who, for centuries unnumbered, have watched and studied all of Time and Space with intellects (as H.G. Wells put it) vast and cool and unsympathetic. Their philosophy was never to interfere in the affairs of alien races, merely to watch and wait.

But one of their number, known only as the Doctor, found such inaction anathema. As he studied the interplay of great forces in the cosmos, the endless wars and invasions, the entropic conflict between Good and Evil, the rights and lives of a thousand alien life forms debased and brutalized, the wrongs left unrighted . . . he was overcome by the compulsion *to act*! He was a renegade, a misfit in the name of justice.

And so he stole a TARDIS and fled.

Ah, yes. The TARDIS. That most marvelous device for spanning the Time-lines and traversing all of known/unknown Space. The name is an acronym for Time And Relative Dimensions In Space. Marvelous! An amazing machine that can change shape to fit in with any locale in which it materializes. But the TARDIS stolen from his fellow Time Lords by the Doctor was in for repairs. And so it was frozen in the shape of its first appearance: a British police call box. Those of you who have been to England may have seen such call boxes. (There are very few of them extant currently, because the London "bobbies" now have two-way radio in their patrol cars; but before the advent of that communication system the tall, dark blue street call box—something like our old-fashioned wooden phone booth—was a familiar sight in the streets of London. If a police officer needed assistance he could call in directly from such a box, and if the station house wanted to get in touch with a copper they could turn on the big blue light atop the box and its flashing would attract a "bobby.")

Further wonder: the outward size of the TARDIS does not reveal its relative size *inside*. The size of a phone booth outwardly, it is enormous within, holding many sections filled with the Doctor's super-scientific equipment.

Unfortunately, the stolen TARDIS needed more repairs than just the fixing of its shape-changing capabilities. Its steering mechanism was also wonky, and so the Doctor could never be certain that the coordinates he set for time and place of materializing would be correct. He might set course for the Planet Karn . . . and wind up in Victorian London. He might wish to relax at an intergalactic pleasure resort . . . and pop into existence in Antarctica. He might lay in a course for the deadly gold mines of Voga . . . and appear in Renaissance Italy.

It makes for a chancy existence, but the Doctor takes it all unflinchingly. As do his attractive female traveling companions, whose liaisons with the Doctor are never sufficiently explicated for those of us with a nasty, suspicious turn of mind.

The Doctor *looks* human and, apart from his quirky way of thinking, even *acts* human most of the time. But he is a Time Lord, not a mere mortal. He has two hearts, a stable body temperature of 60°, and—not to stun you too much—he's approximately 750 years old. Or at least he was that age when the first of the 43 *Doctor Who* novels was written. God (or Time Lords) only knows how old he is now!

Only slightly less popular than the good Doctor himself are his arch-foes and the distressing alien monsters he battles through the pages of these wild books and in phosphor-dot reality on your TV screens. They seem endless in their variety: the Vardans, the Oracle, Fendahl, the virus swarm of the Purpose, The Master, the

Tong of the Black Scorpion, the evil brain of Morbius, the mysterious energy force known as the Mandragora Helix, the android clone Kraals, the Zygons, the Cybermen, the Ice Warriors, the Autons, the spore beast called the Krynoid and—most deadly and menacing of them all—the robot threat of the Daleks.

Created by mad Davros, the great Kaled scientist, the pepper-pot-shaped Daleks made such an impression in England when they were first introduced into the series that they became a cultural artifact almost immediately. Movies have been made about them, toys have been manufactured of Daleks, coloring books, Dalek candies, soaps, slippers, Easter eggs and even special Dalek fireworks. They rival the Doctor for the attention of a fascinated audience and they have been brought back again and again during the fourteen years the series has perpetuated itself on BBC television; and their shiveringly pleasurable manifestations have not been confined just to England and America. *Doctor Who* and the Daleks have millions of rabid fans in over thirty countries around the world.

Like the three fictional characters *every* nation knows—Sherlock Holmes, Tarzan and Superman—Doctor Who seems to have a universal appeal.

Let me conclude this paean of praise with these thoughts: hating *Star Wars* and "Star Trek" is not a difficult chore for me. I recoil from that sophomoric species of creation that excuses its simplistic cliche structure and homage to the transitory (as does *Star Wars*) as violently as I do from that which sententiously purports to be deep and intellectual when it is, in fact, superficial self-conscious twaddle (as does "Star Trek"). This is not to say that I am an ivory tower intellect whose doubledome can only support Proust or Descartes. When I was a little kid, and was reading everything I could lay hands on, I read the classics with joy, but enjoyed equally those works I've come to think of as "elegant trash": the Edgar Rice Burroughs novels, The Shadow, Doc Savage, Conan, comic books and Uncle Wiggly. They taught me a great deal of what I know about courage and truth and ethic in the world.

To that list I add *Doctor Who*. His adventures are sunk to the hips in humanism, decency, solid adventure and simple good reading. They are not classics, make no mistake. They can never touch the illuminative level of Dickens or Mark Twain or Kafka. But they are solid entertainment based on an understanding of Good and Evil in the world. They say to us, "You, too, can be Doctor Who. You, like the good Doctor, can stand up for that which is bright and bold and true. You can shape the world, if you'll only go and try."

And they do it in the form of *all* great literature . . . the cracking good, well-plotted adventure yarn. They are direct lineal heirs to the adventures of Rider Haggard and Talbot Mundy, of H.G. Wells and Jules Verne, of Mary Shelley and Ray Bradbury. They are worth your time.

And if you give yourself up to the Doctor's winsome ways, he will take substance and reality in your imagination. For that reason, for the inestimable goodness and delight in every *Doctor Who* adventure, for the benefits he proffers, I lend my name and my urging to read and watch him.

I don't think you'll do less than thank me for shoving you down with this book in your hands, and telling you . . . here's Who. Meet the Doctor.

The pleasure is all mine. And all yours, kiddo.

HARLAN ELLISON
Los Angeles

DOCTOR WHO
AND THE SEEDS OF DOOM

1

Mystery under the Ice

Everywhere, as far as the eye could see, was a gleaming expanse of white. Moberly adjusted his goggles to counteract the glare and brushed the tiny icicles from his beard. The temperature was dropping fast, and judging from the cloud formation above the distant hills, a blizzard was brewing. Two years in the Antarctic had taught him to pay attention to such signs. He pulled his parka tightly around his face and called to another muffled figure crouched in a deep trench near by.

"Come on, Charles! The weather's turning. We've got enough samples for testing." The other man seemed not to hear him. He was hacking furiously at something in the trench with his ice pick. Moberly dropped down beside him.

"Look," said his companion. He pointed at a dark gourd-like object, about the size of a pineapple, embedded in the icy wall.

"What is it?" asked Moberly, his eyes widening in amazement.

"Dunno. But it's not ice," said the man named Charles, and he carefully prised the object free. "Bit of a mystery, eh?"

Moberly nodded. "Let's get it back to camp and

take a proper look." He took the strange object from Charles and climbed out of the trench. It felt curiously heavy considering its size. He placed it on the sledge and teamed up the dogs for the trek back to camp. Charles joined him a moment later and the two men set off across the icy waste, the dogs barking excitedly. A sudden squall of snow blew across the sledge as it gathered speed and the wind began to howl in the distance. Moberly shivered. Without knowing why, he felt uneasy, as if the approaching blizzard carried with it a sense of impending doom.

The bright yellow huts which formed Antarctica Camp Three sat huddled in the snow at the foot of a low ridge of mountains. The huts were linked by corrugated steel tunnels which gleamed like new whenever the sun shone. Now, however, the air was dark with snow as the blizzard swept down from the mountains. Moberly and his companion, Charles Winlett, had been lucky to reach camp in time.

Inside the huts the contrast was astonishing. The specially insulated walls and ceiling kept the atmosphere at an even temperature and the overall impression was one of warmth and light. In the laboratory, John Stevenson, the expedition's chief botanist, was carefully freeing hardened ice from the outer surface of the pod-like object. He was a pleasant, chubby man of about forty-five, with a gingery moustache and thinning hair. In his white lab coat he had the air of a kindly dentist as he probed the pod with a metal spatula.

He stopped and turned as Winlett and Moberly entered. They had removed their outer furs and were now dressed in jeans and sweaters. Derek

Moberly was a large man with a big bushy beard and a serious expression. He was a zoologist and the most recent arrival on the polar expedition, which had been in the field now for three years. Charles Winlett, a geologist, was smaller and neater with a trim beard and pale blue eyes which twinkled with good humor. Both men were in their early thirties.

Moberly crossed to the pod. "Animal, vegetable or mineral, John?" he asked.

"Vegetable," replied Stevenson without hesitation. "The cutaneous creasing is unmistakable. When it's properly thawed I can confirm it with a cytology test." He gave the pod another poke with his spatula. The ice was already melting in places to reveal a hard green casing. Steveson stared at it, puzzled. "How deep in the permafrost was it?" he asked.

"I'd guess about the ninth layer," replied Winlett, "which means it's been there at least twenty thousand years."

There was a moment's silence as the significance of this remark sank in. All three men were experts in their field but none of them had come up against anything like this before. The pod sat still and silent, glowing strangely in the rays of the ultra-violet lamp being used to thaw it out.

"Well it looks tropical to me, like a gourd," ventured Moberly.

"Rubbish, Derek," said Winlett. "If it's the late Pleistocene period it can't be tropical. It's a few million years since this part of the Antarctica was rain forest."

"That's the accepted theory," said Moberly. "Discoveries like this have destroyed accepted theories before, isn't that right, John?"

Stevenson did not reply. He was staring fixedly at the pod as if in a trance. "Something wrong?" asked Moberly, and he suddenly remembered the feeling of unease that came over him when he first handled the pod himself. Stevenson rubbed his head.

"Don't you feel it?" he said slowly. There was a hint of fear in his voice.

"Feel what?" said Winlett.

"Something odd . . . strange . . . as if . . ." Stevenson struggled for the words, ". . . as if there's some kind of other presence in the room."

Winlett laughed. "You're imagining things, John. Must be that rice pudding you had for lunch."

Stevenson did not smile. "I'm not joking." He crouched over the pod as if mesmerized by it. Winlett and Moberly exchanged glances. They had never seen Stevenson like this before. He was usually cool and level-headed, not given to wild imaginings. What had got into him? Suddenly Stevenson gave a cry and backed away from the pod. "I know what's wrong." His voice dropped to a whisper. "It's alive! That thing is still alive!" He began pushing the others toward the door.

"Wait a minute," said Winlett. "How can you tell?"

"I don't know how, but I'm certain it's a living organism." Stevenson spoke with total conviction. "I'm going to transmit pictures to London. Come on." He strode out of the room. Winlett shrugged his shoulders and followed.

Moberly remained at the door a moment, an anxious look on his face. Although he didn't like to admit it, he too found the pod worrying and somehow frightening. He glanced across at it. It lay there on the bench, silent and sinister, an unwelcome guest from the Earth's deep and hidden past.

By two o'clock that same day pictures of the pod, received direct by satellite from Antarctica, had succeeded in mystifying every botanical expert in England. Sir Colin Thackeray, Head of the World Ecology Bureau, was beginning to think he was the victim of some gigantic hoax. In desperation he had finally told his Deputy, Dunbar, to get on to a chap called the "Doctor" who worked for UNIT (United Nations Intelligence Task Force). "Bit of a long shot," Sir Colin had said, "but worth a try in the circumstances."

It was understandable why Dunbar adopted a sceptical, even sarcastic attitude to the peculiar personage who invaded his office later that afternoon.

Wearing a long red velvet coat, a broad-brimmed hat, and a large multi-colored scarf trailed over his shoulder, the Doctor hardly looked the picture of scientific eminence. Dunbar wondered if in fact this was the man Sir Colin had meant, or whether there had been some mistake. He took the photographs of the pod from the filing cabinet. "I doubt very much if you can help us—er—'Doctor,'" he began frostily. "These pictures have baffled all the experts. The only reasonable explanation seems to be that the pod comes from some extinct species of plant."

The Doctor sprawled into a chair, dumped his feet on Dunbar's desk and beamed a large, friendly smile. "It is the sign of a tiny mind to look for reasonable explanations, Mr. Dunbar. The Universe is full of *un*reasonable things, only capable of being explained *un*reasonably." Dunbar looked uncomfortable at this challenge to the normal processes of thought. "Consider for a moment," continued the Doctor, "the alternative hypothesis." He waved his arm airily.

"Such as," snapped Dunbar, beginning to feel irritated.

"That the pod may have originated in outer space." The Doctor smiled sweetly as if no one but a fool could possibly think otherwise.

Dunbar angrily thrust the photographs at the Doctor. "If you have ever seen anything like this, you must have a very powerful telescope," he said tartly. The Doctor pushed back the brim of his hat and studied the photographs. For the first time Dunbar noticed how blue and penetrating the Doctor's eyes were, and he could not help feeling he was in the presence of a very strange and powerful person, so strange he seemed not quite human.

The Doctor tossed the photos back on the desk. "Mr. Dunbar, how long is it since there was vegetation in Antarctica?"

Dunbar explained this was something the World Ecology expedition was trying to establish. The pod had been found deep in the permafrost, twenty or thirty thousand years under the ice.

"Yes, and it's probably still ticking," interrupted the Doctor. He leapt out of his chair and headed for the door.

"What? I don't understand . . ."

The Doctor stabbed the air with his forefinger. "A time bomb, Mr. Dunbar, a time bomb! Are you in touch with the expedition?"

Dunbar nodded. "A daily video link."

"Good. Tell them to keep a constant guard on

this pod but not to touch it under any circumstances until I arrive."

"You're going out there?" said Dunbar, overcome by the sudden turn of events.

The Doctor bobbed his head back in. "Just as soon as I've picked up my assistant and a toothbrush. And remember—no one must touch that pod!" Before Dunbar could reply again the Doctor had disappeared, like a vanishing rabbit in a conjuring trick.

Dunbar shook his head in disbelief. The last few minutes had been so unlike the ordered calm which usually prevailed in his office, that he was half inclined to doubt whether the preceding interview had really taken place at all. Finally he crossed to his desk and dialed a number on the intercom. "Sir Colin? . . . Dunbar here," he said. "That chap you called in from UNIT . . . is he quite sane?"

It was the middle of the night at Antarctica Camp Three. The blizzard had begun to subside but the wind still whined around the huts. Winlett was sitting in the laboratory near the pod, dozing. The room was in darkness, save for the eerie glow of the ultra-violet lamp. A half empty mug of cocoa stood on the bench where Winlett had left it before falling asleep. Now he was slumped awkwardly in his chair a few feet away. Earlier that day Stevenson had measured the pod and found to everyone's amazement that it had grown five centimeters in circumference. He had immediately ordered a round-the-clock vigil to monitor its progress. Winlett knew that such growth defied all normal biological laws. The pod had no root system to feed with and no nitrogen intake. It was odd, and disturbing. He had wondered whether Stevenson was right to continue the ultra-violet radiation in view of the warning from London, but Stevenson had brushed these fears aside.

A distant door banged shut with the wind and Winlett stirred. Still half-asleep, he shifted his position in the chair, bringing an arm to rest on the bench not far from the pod. Then he dozed off again.

Suddenly, with no sound whatsoever, the pod began to vibrate and tiny cracks appeared in the outer casing. It was opening! Winlett remained asleep and unaware.

From the top of the pod emerged a green tendril, like the shoot of some exotic plant. It reared several feet in the air then slowly turned its head, like a deadly snake seeking its victim. Seconds later it sensed the presence of another living creature in the room. Gradually, the tendril crept toward Winlett. Then, in one quick motion, it engulfed his arm. Winlett jerked awake with a cry of pain. In blind panic he reeled across the room clutching his arm. The tendril had detached itself from the pod and was clinging to him.

"John! Derek!" he shouted desperately, but a strange, cold sensation was already rushing through his body. He felt weak, his knees crumpled, and a terrible darkness descended in his brain.

2

Death Stalks the Camp

After his interview with the Doctor, Dunbar did not go straight home. Instead, he drove thirty miles out of London, taking particular care he was not followed, to pay a visit on someone very special.

"Mr. Richard Dunbar, sir, of the World Ecology Bureau." The butler threw open a pair of metal studded doors and Dunbar entered the room.

"Room" was hardly the word to describe the place he now found himself in. Dunbar literally gasped with shock at the sight. For all around him, on each side, were nothing but plants—plants of every description; creepers, suckers, lichen, fungi, giant rubber plants, monstrous cacti, rare tropical blossoms, trailing vines, bamboo—the room was a living jungle, a Sargasso Sea of waving green. Dunbar guessed it must be at least fifty yards long, although the farthest walls were invisible. High above, he could just make out a vaulted ceiling through the thick foliage.

A raised iron walkway ran down the center of the room and at the far end a man was spraying an exotic-looking flower with loving care. He was dressed immaculately in a dark Savile Row suit, and his hands were covered by elegant black leather gloves.

The man turned as the butler made his announcement and glided down the catwalk toward Dunbar. He stopped and stared, without speaking. His eyes were extraordinarily large, like those of a predatory cat.

"Mr. Chase?" said Dunbar. "Mr. Harrison Chase?"

The man nodded. There was something menacing about him. Lean and panther-like, he had the unmistakable stamp of power. A man not to be trifled with. A man who would stop at nothing to get his own way.

He spoke. "And what is your Bureau doing about bonsai?"

"Bonsai?"

"Mutilation and torture, Mr. Dunbar. The hideous Japanese practice of miniaturizing shrubs and trees."

"We try to conserve all animal and plant life," replied Dunbar hurriedly.

"I'm glad to hear it." The cat's eyes flashed dangerously. "I consider it my mission in life to protect the plant life of Mother Earth. And she needs a protector, does she not?"

Dunbar agreed. He knew of this man's obsession with plants, knew too that he was a millionaire many times over, with a considerable private army in his employ. It was wiser to agree than disagree with such a man. He fumbled with his briefcase and took out a large buff envelope.

"I have come to show you something. Mr. Chase, something discovered by one of our expeditions." He undid the envelope and handed over the photographs. "A mysterious, unidentified pod."

Chase examined the photographs. "Very interesting. Where was it found?"

Dunbar hesitated. This was the moment he had been waiting for, the moment he would gamble not only his career but, if the rumors about Chase were true, perhaps even his life.

"In the Antarctic, under our control," he replied finally. "But of course, in our violent and uncertain world, Mr. Chase, anything can happen . . ." He paused. "Such a valuable specimen could easily disappear . . . for a price." He looked hesitantly into the dark, feline eyes.

"I want the precise location."

Dunbar reached into his case again. "A map and all the information you require."

Chase smiled. "Such forethought, Mr. Dunbar. An excellent attribute, and one for which you will be well rewarded." He clapped his hands. "Hargreaves, call Scorby in here, and show Mr. Dunbar out."

The butler bowed wordlessly and ushered Dunbar into the corridor. The audience was over.

Alone, Chase stared hungrily at the photographs once more. "Unique! The only plant of its kind in the world," he whispered. "*Compositae Harrison Chase*! Yes, I must have it. I must!" The cat-like eyes gleamed bright and manic.

A noise at the door broke the spell.

"You wanted me, Mr. Chase?" The speaker was a tall, swarthy man with a pointed black beard.

"Yes, Scorby. I'm sending you on a little errand. You'd better take Keeler with you. Oh, and wrap up well. It could be snowing."

Sarah Jane Smith had never felt so cold in her life. She was already regretting this mad trip to Antarctica. After two years as the Doctor's special assistant she should have known better, she told herself.

She drew the hood of her parka tight and glanced across at the Doctor. He remained impassive, staring out of the helicopter window. He was being unusually secretive about their mission. A sure sign he was worried, decided Sarah.

Suddenly the pilot yelled above the engine noise. "There she is!"

The helicopter began to turn and drop. Beneath them Sarah could just make out a huddle of bright yellow huts. So this was Antarctica Camp Three. Not exactly the center of civilization.

They landed and Sarah leapt out after the Doctor. The big blades swirled dangerously overhead, creating a miniature snowstorm. A figure ran out from one of the huts to greet them.

"Welcome to the loneliest spot on Earth. You must be the Doctor. We were expecting someone a lot older."

The Doctor smiled. "I'm only seven hundred and forty-nine. I used to be even younger."

The man grinned, not knowing how to take this remark. He turned to Sarah and extended a hand. "Derek Moberly, how do you do?"

"Sarah Jane Smith, the *young* Doctor's assistant," she laughed. "Tell me, is the weather always like this? I feel I've got frostbite already."

Moberly chuckled. "No, sometimes it gets quite warm. Ten degrees below freezing." He eyed the Doctor's red velvet frock-coat. "Are you all right dressed like that?"

"I haven't traveled ten thousand miles to discuss the weather," snapped the Doctor. "Shall we get started?"

A few minutes later he stood next to Stevenson in

the Sick Bay, gazing down at the motionless form of Winlett.

"He hasn't spoken a word since last night," explained Stevenson anxiously. "We heard a cry, came in and found him on the laboratory floor. The pod was open."

The Doctor glanced at the progress chart and raised an eyebrow in surprise. "According to these figures he should be dead." He pulled back the bedclothes.

Stevenson gasped in horror. "Good grief! What is it?"

Winlett's right hand had completely vanished and in its place was a green, vegetable-like growth.

"Whatever came out of that pod has obviously infected him," replied the Doctor grimly. "How soon can you get a proper medical team here?"

Stevenson tugged at his moustache. "We've been on to them, but conditions are bad. Maybe tomorrow."

The Doctor straightened the bedclothes and stepped back. "I doubt if tomorrow is going to be soon enough. Show me the pod."

Stevenson led him out of the Sick Bay and down a narrow, corrugated steel tunnel to a door marked "Laboratory." Inside, Sarah and Moberly were huddled over a crackling radio set.

"What is it?" asked Stevenson.

"Bad news," said Moberly gravely. "The medical team has turned back. One of their Snocats fell into a crevasse."

Stevenson began to panic. "What are we going to do? Winlett's dying."

"No he's not," said the Doctor. "He's changing form, which could be worse. We need a blood test. Fast."

"I'm a zoologist. I can prepare a specimen slide," offered Moberly.

The Doctor nodded. "Right." Moberly hurried out and the Doctor turned to Stevenson. "The pod?"

Stevenson led him to the bench where the pod had lain open and untouched since the attack on Winlett. The Doctor stooped to examine it. "Why did it open, I wonder?" he muttered to himself.

Stevenson shifted uneasily. "That could be my fault. I used the ultra-violet lamp to thaw it out. I felt certain there was life there, you see."

The Doctor rose and gave him a stony stare. "Mr. Stevenson," he said slowly and deliberately, "what you have done could result in the total destruction of life on this planet."

In the Sick Bay Winlett was growing worse by the minute, as the green infection crept relentlessly up his arm.

Meanwhile, the Doctor had asked to see the trench where the pod had been found. For over an hour, he, Stevenson and Sarah had battled through a howling gale to reach the spot. Now he was digging furiously in the icy wall with a small pick, oblivious to the biting wind and thick snow which almost blotted the other two from view.

Suddenly he stopped. "Yes, I thought so. Here we are." He threw the pick aside and, scrabbling with his bare hands, lifted out of the ice a second pod, an exact replica of the first.

"Another pod!" gasped Sarah.

"How did you know . . ." began Stevenson. "Will there be any more?"

"No. They always travel in pairs. Like policemen." The Doctor stood up, clearly very pleased with himself.

"What are we going to do with it?" asked Sarah, puzzled.

"Put it in the fridge. Come on." The Doctor scrambled out of the trench. The other two followed, none the wiser.

It was almost nightfall by the time they regained Camp. The Doctor immediately placed the pod in a special freeze box in the lab, used for keeping ice samples. There was no further news on the medical team but Moberly had taken the blood test. One look confirmed the Doctor's suspicions. The platelets of Winlett's blood—magnified a thousandfold—revealed the presence of plant bacteria.

"As I thought," said the Doctor, removing his eye from the microscope, "a human being whose blood is turning into vegetable soup!"

At that moment the roar of an aircraft engine shook the walls of the Crew Quarters where they were standing.

"The medical team!" cried Sarah jubilantly.

"Quick, Derek, the landing lights!" yelled Stevenson, and the two of them grabbed their snowsuits and dashed outside.

Sarah turned to the Doctor. "Will they be able to do anything for that man?"

"I don't know, Sarah. He's half way toward becoming a Krynoid."

"Krynoid?"

The Doctor nodded.

"You mean you recognized the pod?"

"Oh yes," said the Doctor. "I was fairly certain when I saw the photographs in London. But now I'm sure."

"Well, what is a Krynoid?" demanded Sarah.

peeved he had not told her of his suspicions. "What does it do?"

"You could describe it as a galactic weed," explained the Doctor. "The pod we found is just one of a thousand seeds dispersed by the mother plant. Given the right conditions, each pod releases a parasitic shoot which attaches itself to the nearest animal life-form—in this instance it happened to be human. The infected victim changes rapidly and ultimately develops into a fully grown Krynoid, thus completing the cycle."

Sarah gasped. "But that's terrifying! How did these pods manage to land here on Earth?"

"Good question," said the Doctor, tapping the side of his nose. "I wish I knew the answer. Possibly their planet of origin is very turbulent. Every so often there could be internal explosions which send surface matter shooting off into space." He paused, as if weighing up the pros and cons of the theory in his mind.

The door burst open at this point and Moberly and Stevenson struggled in, supporting two frozen, semi-collapsed figures.

"Is this the medical team?" asked the Doctor.

"Afraid not," gasped Stevenson as he helped ease the two strangers gently into a couple of chairs. "Just got themselves lost."

Moberly administered some piping hot coffee from a flask, which the two men gratefully gulped down.

"Sorry to be such a nuisance," said one of them finally. "We were running low on fuel when we saw your lights." He was tall and swarthy, with a black pointed beard.

"That was lucky," said Sarah. "Lights are few and far between in Antarctica."

The Doctor's voice, urgent and decisive, cut through these explanations. "The medical team was our last chance. Now we must act for ourselves. And quickly." He shot out of the room.

"Where's he going now?" asked Stevenson.

"Where do you think?" replied Sarah. "Come on." She hurried out, Stevenson and Moberly close behind her.

Left alone, the two strangers exchanged wary glances.

"Do you think they swallowed it?" said the second man. He was small and ferrety.

"Don't worry, Keeler," said the dark one. "What can they do?" He tapped his left breast and grinned. The bulge of an automatic pistol could just be seen beneath his nylon snowsuit.

The Doctor was already in the Sick Bay when Sarah and the others rushed in. They were totally unprepared for the sight which hit them. Winlett lay on the bed, deathly pale, his breath rasping and distorted. The plant-like infection now covered his entire right side.

Stevenson fought for words. "It's . . . it's as if he's turning into some kind of monster!"

"That's exactly what is happening," said the Doctor gravely.

"Can't we do anything to help?"

"Yes, but it's drastic," warned the Doctor. "We can amputate the arm. It's his only chance."

"But none of us are surgeons," protested Moberly. "It could be fatal."

"It's a risk we have to take," snapped the Doctor. "Come on!" He led the way out.

The door shut on the motionless form in the bed. For a few seconds everything remained still as the footsteps receded up the corridor. Then, slowly, the figure of Winlett sat up, his head swiveled trance-like toward the door, and the glazed lifeless eyes stared murderously out of their sockets.

In the lab the Doctor was issuing orders. "Sarah, we'll need hot water and towels! Stevenson, get more lights. Moberly, you have some medical training. You can perform the actual surgery."

Moberly nodded and started to gather equipment and instruments onto a tray. The Doctor glanced at the clock above the door. Every second was vital. Not only Winlett's life was at stake. Once the Krynoid organism was allowed to take root in one person, it was merely a matter of time before the whole of humanity fell prey to the lethal weed.

Moberly finished his preparations and made for the door. "I'll take these to the Sick Bay and start setting up."

"Good man," said the Doctor.

Sarah glanced anxiously in his direction. "Do you think there's a chance?"

"There's always a chance," said the Doctor quietly, but Sarah could tell he was worried.

Moberly walked carefully down the tunnel. The Doctor was right, they would need more lights. He hoped Stevenson could fix the transformer or something. He turned the corner near the Sick Bay. That was odd! The door was open. He crept forward the last few paces and peered in. The bed was empty.

"Charles?" There was no reply. "Charles, where are you?"

Moberly stepped into the room and put down the tray. As he did so something strange and cold, like a piece of wet seaweed, touched the back of his neck. He spun around. A hideous, semi-human shape lunged at his throat and started to throttle him. Gasping, Moberly sank to his knees. The pressure increased. He couldn't breathe! The room began to spin, everything was going blurred, he could not escape from the suffocating grip! Then, nothing but blackness, rushing and overwhelming . . .

Moberly fell to the floor, dead. The dark, monstrous shape rose from his body, glided like a phantom down the murky passage and slipped into the howling, stormy night outside.

3

Hunt in the Snow

Carrying an armful of towels and fresh linen, Sarah made her way toward the Sick Bay. As she drew near she suddenly felt a cold draught around her feet. Someone must have left an outside door open. She turned the corner and froze with horror. There, slumped in the shadows, lay the body of Moberly. One glance was enough to tell her the worst. She spun around. The door at the far end of the passage was banging on its hinges in the wind and snow had started to drift in. She shut the door and hurried back to the lab.

"Moberly's dead." Sarah stood framed in the doorway, white as a ghost.

"What?" cried Stevenson.

The Doctor threw aside the tray of bottles he was preparing and darted out. In two seconds he was by the body. There was a faint green mark under the chin. "I found an outside door open," said Sarah. "Something must have come in."

"No, Sarah," said the Doctor chillingly. "Something went out."

He entered the Sick Bay. The bed lay empty and all around were clear signs that a struggle had taken place.

Stevenson shook his head. "You don't mean Charles . . ."

". . . left after killing Moberly," finished the Doctor. "Only he is no longer Charles. He is an alien."

"An alien? I can't believe it," cried Stevenson in anguish.

"I told you he was changing form. Already his mind has been taken over. Eventually his entire body will alter."

"Into a Krynoid?" said Sarah.

The Doctor nodded and turned to Stevenson. "Winlett as you knew him is already dead. For the sake of the rest of humanity we must destroy what he had become." He spoke gently but with finality.

Stevenson lowered his eyes, believing but not wanting to accept this terrible truth.

In the Crew Quarters the stranger with a beard was methodically searching the room. He found a rifle under one of the bunks and began to dismantle it.

"What are you doing, Scorby?" His companion spoke nervously.

"I don't like guns . . . in the wrong hands." Scorby tampered with the firing pin for a few minutes and, satisfied the mechanism was sabotaged, replaced the rifle carefully under the bunk.

"I wish you'd stop acting like some cheap gangster. We've only come here to confirm the pod is something unusual."

Scorby grinned. "You don't think we're going to fly back empty-handed, do you, Keeler?"

The small man looked genuinely surprised. "It's the first you've mentioned . . . what are you planning?"

Scorby gave a nasty leer. "Tomorrow we dig a nice big hole in the snow—big enough for, say, five bodies. Then we fill the hole, take the pod and go home . . . No witnesses, nothing. Just another lost expedition."

Keeler recoiled in disgust. "You're mad! I won't do that!"

"You'll do exactly as you're told," Scorby tapped his pistol threateningly, "Or else . . . I'll just make that hole a little bigger."

Keeler back away and nearly collided with the Doctor as he came hurtling in, followed by Sarah and Stevenson.

"Come on! We don't have much time," the Doctor sounded impatient. Sarah and Stevenson hurriedly donned their snowsuits.

"What's the trouble?" asked Scorby, quickly regaining his composure.

"We're going out."

"In this weather?"

"Yes, in this weather," snapped the Doctor.

Stevenson crossed to his bunk and took out the rifle. "Ready!"

The Doctor eyed the weapon. "I hope that's the answer," he said quietly, and led the way out.

Keeler turned anxiously on Scorby as the door slammed. "What the devil's going on?"

"I don't know. They're not going to build a snowman, that's for sure." He stepped over to the door. "Come on. Now's our chance."

"What do you mean?"

"To find the pod." He opened the door gently and, checking the corridor was clear, beckoned Keeler to follow.

* * *

Outside, it was very dark and a heavy snow was falling. Sarah noticed that although they had only traveled a few hundred yards the lights of the camp behind them were no longer visible. She shivered. The cold was already unbearable and constant flurries of snow prevented her from seeing more than a few feet ahead. She stumbled on behind the Doctor. He seemed oblivious to the conditions, pausing only once in a while to secure his hat. All the time he was scanning the endless expanse of snow.

"No sign of any tracks," yelled Sarah.

Stevenson shook his head. "The wind covers everything in a matter of minutes."

Suddenly the Doctor pointed. "What's that over there?" They had reached a high ridge and he was gazing at something below.

Stevenson peered into the gloom. "That's our Power Unit." A small metal building lay half-buried in the snow, several hundred yards distant. Only the Doctor's superhuman eyesight could have picked it out from such a range.

"Why is it so far from the camp?" he shouted.

"Safety measure. It's a new fuel-cell system. Being tested out here for the first time."

"Let's take a look!"

They scrambled down the ice-covered slope and approached the Power Unit. The snow seemed undisturbed.

"This door can't have been opened for weeks," remarked Sarah. "It's iced solid."

"It's as well to be sure," said the Doctor and he started to yank it open. "He'd try to find shelter in this weather." Stevenson slipped the safety catch on his rifle. After a couple of hefty pulls from the

Doctor the ice cracked away and the three of them stepped inside.

The walls and floor of the Power Unit were bare, but in the center stood a large complicated structure, about ten feet across, giving out a soft glow of heat. This was the experimental fuel cell. One or two large pipes and cables ran off to the walls and then underground to the rest of the camp, to supply the power and electricity needed. There was very little scope for concealment.

"No cactus spines or puddles of snow," said Sarah. "Doesn't look like he's been here."

"Is there anywhere else he could hide?" the Doctor asked Stevenson.

"Not outside the camp itself."

"He wouldn't last long, would he . . . outside?" ventured Sarah.

"Not without special clothing," replied Stevenson. "No, I'm afraid Charles must have collapsed somewhere."

"You keep forgetting, Stevenson—he isn't a man any more. Not of flesh and blood."

"Well, if he's a plant, Doctor—or a vegetable, whatever he is—he'd have even less resistance to cold, wouldn't he?" argued Sarah.

"Perhaps. On the other hand, the Krynoid might come from a planet where this would be considered glorious summer."

Stevenson frowned. "You know, I still find this hard to take. You're trying to tell me these things are an alien plant species?"

"And lethal to all human and animal life."

"But how do you know?"

"Never mind how I know, it's fact. On every planet where the Krynoid gets established all animal life is extinguished. What happened to your friend Moberly should convince you." Sarah could see the Doctor was irritated by Stevenson. She tried to sound reassuring.

"But there's no real danger now, is there? One pod is safely in the freezer and . . ." she was about to say "Winlett" but checked herself, "and . . . the other . . . is probably frozen stiff under the snow."

The Doctor crossed to the door. "I hope you're right, Sarah," he said as he led them out.

The three figures emerging from the Power Unit were unaware of a hideous form crouched behind a snowbank, less than twenty feet away. Its cold, inhuman eyes followed the Doctor's movements as he bolted the door from the outside. Then, as the trio climbed back up the ridge and out of sight, the creature—half man, half plant—crept from hiding and crawled across the snow toward the building. With one swift movement it prised open the door and entered. Inside, it let out a low rattling noise and settled beside the fuel cell, sucking in the warmth.

In the laboratory, Scorby and Keeler were conducting a methodical search.

"You're supposed to be the botanist, Keeler. Where would you keep this pod?"

"It must be here somewhere." Keeler looked around in desperation. Scorby picked up an intricate piece of measuring equipment and held it aloft. "Careful!" warned his companion, "that's valuable."

Scorby grinned, then smashed it violently onto the floor. "So what?" he sneered, "there'll be nobody here to use it after we leave."

Suddenly the radio sprang to life. "HELLO . . .

HELLO . . . THIS IS SOUTH BEND CALLING CAMP THREE . . . COME IN CAMP THREE . . . OVER . . ."

Scorby darted a look at Keeler then crossed to the radio. He pressed a switch. "Camp Three receiving you. . . over."

"IS THAT YOU DEREK?" said the voice, distorted by static.

Scorby hesitated. "Er . . . yes . . . go ahead, South Bend."

The voice continued. "THE WEATHER'S CLEARING THIS END. THE MEDICAL TEAM WILL BE WITH YOU AS SOON AS POSSIBLE."

"Have they left yet?" asked Scorby, concealing his alarm.

"THEY'RE LEAVING RIGHT NOW."

"Cancel them!" ordered Scorby. "We don't need help. Everything's under control."

There was silence for a moment, then the voice spoke again, this time inquisitive and suspicious. "HELLO? . . . IS THAT YOU DEREK?"

Smiling, Scorby clicked off the radio and began smashing the circuits with the butt of his gun. Keeler looked up in alarm.

"What are you doing?"

"Fixing it," grinned Scorby. "Didn't anyone ever tell you, silence is golden?"

"But . . ."

"Shut up, Keeler, and find that pod!" The small man winced as his partner savagely dismembered the radio equipment.

A few moments later, however, Keeler let out an excited yell as he removed a tray from under the bench. On it lay the two empty halves of the first pod.

"Look! It's the pod in Dunbar's photograph." He fitted the two halves together.

"Some idiot's cut it open," hissed Scorby.

Keeler shook his head. "No. It wasn't cut. It must have germinated."

"What's that?"

"The pod has opened as part of its natural cycle to release a shoot or something."

Scorby digested this unexpected piece of information. "But it's the actual *plant* that Harrison Chase wants, right?"

"Right."

"Then what have they done with it, Keeler?" He paced the room nervously. "We've got to find it or Chase'll skin us alive!"

"If you hadn't smashed the radio perhaps we could have asked South Bend."

Scorby gave Keeler a scornful look. "Are you trying to be funny? The discovery of this pod has been kept secret. Only the top brass of the Ecology Bureau know about it."

"And Harrison Chase," corrected Keeler.

"That bloke on the radio said medical aid was coming. Medical aid for who? There must be someone here who's ill." A malevolent smile settled on his dark features. "And he'll tell us where this thing is, I promise you."

Gun in hand, Scorby led the way out of the lab and down the passage. It ran to an intersection.

"Which way?" whispered Keeler.

Scorby paused then headed to his left. On the floor at the far end of the tunnel was a towel dropped earlier by Sarah in her haste. The two men turned the corner. Opposite was a door marked "Sick Bay." Scorby smiled and pushed open the door. His expression immediately turned to shock as he caught sight of a body on the bed, hurriedly draped in a sheet.

"Is he dead?" gasped Keeler.

Scorby pulled back the sheet. "Stiff as a board."

"Look! What's that?" Keeler's finger pointed to the green mark on Moberly's throat.

"Dunno. But it's not measles." Scorby twitched the sheet back. "And he won't be telling us anything either."

At that moment they both heard a noise in the corridor outside. Footsteps and voices were approaching. Scorby signaled Keeler to go behind the door and quickly positioned himself at the other side. It sounded like the Doctor and that girl. They were bound to notice the open door. Scorby's finger tightened on the trigger of his gun.

The Doctor paused outside the Sick Bay, puzzled. Something was wrong. He motioned to Sarah to keep quiet. Why was the door open? His mind raced through the events of the last few hours like a computer. The two strangers! Of course! Their landing here was too much of a coincidence. They had come with a purpose, and that could mean only one thing!

The Doctor sprang into the room . . . and Scorby's pistol dug coldly into his neck.

4

Sabotage!

"Put your hands up, Doctor!"

The Doctor obeyed.

"And you!"

Sarah was yanked into the room and forced to follow suit.

The Doctor eyed the gun. "Have we annoyed you in some way? Food not to your liking?"

"Shut up!" commanded Scorby viciously. "OK . . . now start talking."

"Make up your mind," smiled the Doctor.

"I said talk."

"Certainly. Did you know that Wolfgang Amadeus Mozart had perfect pitch?"

Sarah could see Scorby was not amused.

"What happened to him?" he hissed, jerking his head toward the bed.

"Wolfgang Amadeus?" The Doctor feigned puzzlement. "Oh, *him*," suddenly serious. "He died."

"We gathered that."

"What did it?" asked Keeler.

The Doctor did not answer.

"It's something to do with that pod, isn't it? What's happened to the pod?"

"What pod?"

The pistol dug deeper into the Doctor's neck. "There's already one corpse in here, Doctor. I can easily double that number."

Sarah glanced anxiously at the Doctor out of the corner of her eye. She felt certain Scorby meant what he said.

Finally the Doctor spoke. "There's been an accident. One of the men here has been . . . infected."

"By the pod?" exclaimed Keeler.

"He went mad," said Sarah quietly.

"Yes," added the Doctor, "you could say he's not quite himself anymore."

"Where is he now?"

"We don't know," answered Sarah. "Somewhere out there."

Keeler glanced around nervously. "You mean you have a homicidal maniac on the loose?"

"More dangerous than that, I'm afraid," replied the Doctor. "If he . . . or rather it, is still alive, then it will be desperate to reach food and warmth. And there's only one place it can find these things." He weighed his words carefully and looked for their effect on the two strangers.

"You mean this camp?"

"Yes, comforting thought, isn't it?" said the Doctor airily. "I advise you to keep all doors and windows locked. That is, if you're planning to stay." He smiled sweetly, like a benevolent hotel proprietor.

Keeler looked anxiously at his partner. "What are we going to do?" Sarah could see the other man was not convinced.

"I want some more answers. But not in here." Scorby nodded toward the bed. "He gives me the creeps. Come on, you two. *Move!*" He prodded the Doctor and Sarah out of the Sick Bay and into the corridor.

* * *

In the Power Unit the creature was growing stronger by the minute, bathed by the warm glow from the fuel cell. All vestige of humanity had long since disappeared and it was now a mass of tendrils and fibrous shoots, like some giant, malformed plant; but a plant that could move and crush and kill. Slowly, it began to stir. From where the green growth was thickest there came a strange, low rattling sound. Then, the whole monstrous shape started to creep toward the door.

The Doctor and Sarah were led into the Crew Quarters and bound hand and foot on the floor. So far the two men seemed to have forgotten about Stevenson, who was busy locking the doors and windows of the outer huts. The Doctor wondered how long it would be before he returned. Stevenson still had his rifle with him. If they could play for time . . . He became aware of Scorby's pistol again.

"Right, Doctor, let's have the truth. Where's the plant that came out of that pod?"

"That grew in the bed that was part of the house that Jack built?"

"I am not a patient man," threatened Scorby.

Suddenly Keeler interrupted. "Ssshh! Hold it. Someone's coming. Must be the other guy."

Scorby turned from the Doctor and pointed his gun at the closed door.

"Doctor? Miss Smith? Where are you?" came a voice from outside.

The door opened and Stevenson entered.

"Come and join the party." Scorby lowered his pistol to wave the visitor in. Stevenson reacted like lightning and fired his rifle point blank at Scorby's chest. There was a harmless click.

Scorby chuckled. "Not very friendly." He grabbed Stevenson by the shoulders and hurled him across the room. "Get over there!" Stevenson fell with a crunch beside the others.

"Good try," said the Doctor.

"What's happening?"

"For some reason these two want to get their hands on the pod." He looked meaningfully at Stevenson. "I've told them how dangerous . . ."

"The pod's still safe?" interrupted Stevenson, misunderstanding. "They haven't taken it out?"

Scorby's ears pricked up visibly and Stevenson realized his blunder.

"Taken it out where?" Scorby turned to Keeler, a look of triumph on his face. "Know what that means?"

Keeler grinned. "They've got a second pod!" Stevenson shot the Doctor an anguished look.

Scroby crossed to them both. "Where is it?"

"Don't be a bigger fool than you already are," said the Doctor angrily. "Don't you understand, it's dangerous!"

"Where is the pod?"

The gun pointed menacingly at them, but the Doctor and Stevenson remained mute.

"Stubborn pair, aren't they," said Scorby, controlling his venom. "All right . . ." He put the pistol against Sarah's head. "I mean it this time," he whispered softly. Sarah felt her stomach turn over. She held her breath for what seemed an eternity.

The Doctor's voice broke the silence. "It's in the freezer."

"Thank you, Doctor." Scorby took out a second, smaller pistol, which he handed to Keeler. "Watch them. You," he prodded Stevenson, "come with me." He bundled the unhappy scientist out of the room.

Keeler trained the gun nervously on the Doctor and Sarah. "Don't worry," beamed the Doctor. "You're quite safe with us."

Stevenson led Scorby to the lab and produced the second pod out of the freezer.

Scorby cursed Keeler under his breath for missing it. "Are there any more?"

"No. This is unique—priceless—as you are no doubt aware."

"What's to stop it breaking open like the other one?"

"It's quite safe at this temperature," replied Stevenson calmly.

"I see. Well, it's going on a little journey, so find me something to keep it cool."

Stevenson hunted around the debris until he found a thermo-container in which he placed the pod. As they returned to the Crew Quarters, Scorby asked about their source of electrical supply. Stevenson explained curtly about the Power Unit.

When they rejoined the others, Stevenson was bound hand and foot like the Doctor and Sarah.

"You can say your good-byes now," sneered Scorby and pointed his gun at the helpless captives.

"You're not going to shoot us in cold blood?" murmured Sarah.

With a laugh Scorby let his arm drop. "No. I've got a better idea." He grabbed hold of Sarah. "You're coming with us. Give me a hand, Keeler." Sarah's feet were untied and she was dragged toward the door.

"How do you expect to get away from here?"

yelled Stevenson. "You said your plane was grounded."

Scorby smiled. "You shouldn't believe everything people tell you." With a bang the door slammed shut.

Sarah, her hands still tied, was led to an outer door.

"Right," ordered Scorby. "Take us to the Power Unit."

"I don't know where you mean," lied Sarah.

"Don't try to be clever. You checked it earlier. Now move!" He shoved her forward into the snow. Keeler followed, carrying the precious container. The trio rounded the corner of the farthest hut and set off across the open waste. It was still snowing, but the first few streaks of dawn were beginning to lighten the sky. Sarah wondered briefly if she would live to see another day.

Inside the Crew Quarters the Doctor had wriggled to his feet and was hopping up and down like a jack-in-a-box. Above his head hung an old hurricane lamp for use in emergencies. Stevenson observed the Doctor's antics in puzzlement.

"What are you doing?"

"Ever played football?" gasped the Doctor, as he headed the lamp off its hook and on to the floor. The glass smashed into fragments. "Quick!"

Stevenson inched over to the Doctor whose fingers had grabbed a piece of the broken glass. "Now keep very still, or I might cut a blood vessel." The Doctor began to saw away at the rope around Stevenson's wrists.

Outside in the cold dawn, the creature observed

the lights of the camp from behind a hillock of snow. It was now seven or eight feet high. After a moment or two, it set off toward the camp, moving at exceptional speed, its long fibrous tentacles dragging behind in the snow. It reached the nearest hut and began to edge slowly along the side looking for a way in.

The trek across the snowy waste seemed to Sarah like a march to the guillotine, an inexorable journey to certain death. Once inside the Power Unit, Scorby tied her to a heavy pipe on the wall and then started to fix an explosive device to the side of the fuel cell.

"This bomb will set off a fault in the system which in trun will blow up the entire camp, leaving no clues whatsoever. Ingenious, don't you think?"

"You're twisted . . . evil!" replied Sarah. "Why kill us all? Why not just take the pod?"

Scorby leered sadistically. "You know too much." He finished wiring the charge and picked up the pod container. "Come on, Keeler, let's get airborne."

Sarah suddenly noticed Keeler's strange, tortured expression. "No . . . no . . . I can't let you do this!" He lunged at Scorby. "It's cold-blooded murder!"

Scorby brushed him aside. "Too late," he snarled. "I've already started the countdown." He turned to Sarah. "You won't have long to wait. Ten minutes at the most." He strode out. Keeler shot Sarah a final, anguished look, then hurried after.

The door slammed shut and Sarah heard the bolt drawn across. She glanced at the detonator. The numerals on the clock were clearly visible. They read five hundred and eighty seconds. She struggled to free her bonds but knew it was hopeless.

With a final wrench the Doctor released his wrists from the biting rope and headed for the door. "I'll get after the pod . . . and Sarah," he snapped at Stevenson. "You contact Main Base on the radio and see if they can intercept the aircraft."

"What about the Krynoid?"

"We'll have to take a chance on that," cried the Doctor and dashed out. Stevenson hobbled after him into the corridor, rubbing his wrists and ankles.

The Doctor set out from the camp at a run, his eyes scanning the murky gray landscape. "Sarah! Sarah!" His voice died on the wind. Although it was nearly daylight the snowfall was still heavy. He hesitated a moment then headed in the direction of the landing strip. They had probably made straight for the plane. It was a slim chance, but he might still be able to stop them taking off.

In the lab, Stevenson was feverishly plugging up the radio. "Hello Main Base . . . hello Main Base . . . can you hear me? . . . Over." The line seemed dead. "Hello Main Base? Over." Nothing.

Behind him the door began to open slowly and a fibrous tentacle pushed its way into the room.

"Hello . . . this is Camp Three calling Main Base. Can you hear me . . . can you hear me?" He threw down the headphones and inspected the back of the equipment. Immediately he saw the damage.

"Sabotage!" he whispered to himself. Then suddenly he realized he was not alone. He whirled around. A terrifying mass of green tentacles was bearing down on him.

"No . . . no . . . !" Stevenson stumbled back, crashing into the radio. But there was no escape. The tentacles were all around him and closing in. He let out a last desperate cry as the Krynoid enveloped him totally.

In the Power Unit, Sarah stared mesmerized as the seconds ticked away.

The Doctor pounded through the snow, his scarf flailing in the wind. What a fool he had been. The pod stolen by a thug with a gun! The consequences were incalculable.

All at once a fresh noise cut through the howl of the wind. The Doctor stopped and strained his ears. It was a plane taking off. He was too late. The thought stabbed him like a knife. Sarah? He hardly dared contemplate her fate. He turned back toward the camp, a lonely and dejected figure. His gaze swept the glaring white snowscape but took nothing in.

Then, abruptly, he jerked to life again. Looming out of the snow a few hundred yards away was the dark shape of the Power Unit building. He set off toward it at full pelt.

Not far away, but hidden by the ridge, another figure also moved quickly through the snow. But this figure was not human, and its purpose was deadly.

Click . . . click . . . click . . . The dial showed less than a minute to go. Sarah felt the panic rise inside her as the ropes refused to give. Suddenly she heard a scrabbling outside the door. Her heart missed a beat. Then it was flung open and the

Doctor burst in. With one bound he was by her side and untying the ropes.

"Doctor! The whole camp is going to be blown sky high any second!" Expertly the Doctor unraveled Sarah's knots and took in the bomb with a hurried glance. There was no time to defuse it.

Sarah pulled one arm free. "Where's Stevenson?"

"I'll have to try and save him." The Doctor released her other arm and hauled Sarah to her feet. "Come on!"

Sarah took one pace and froze. "Doctor, *look*!" She pointed to the door. The Doctor spun around. Blocking the doorway was the monstrous bulk of the Krynoid. From its body sprouted a hundred tentacles, each as thick as a man's arm. Where once a face had existed there was now a gnarled and twisted mass of bark. It remained in the doorway, swaying from side to side and emitting a low, unearthly rattle.

"Get behind me," whispered the Doctor. Sarah did so. She could hear the bomb ticking quite clearly.

The Krynoid started to advance. The Doctor edged around the wall. Suddenly the creature rushed toward them. The Doctor side-stepped, pulling Sarah with him, and one of the green tentacles caught on the metal grid protecting the fuel cell. There was a flash and the Krynoid roared in pain.

"Run!" yelled the Doctor and bundled Sarah toward the door. As she passed the creature Sarah felt a cold, slimy tentacle brush her face. She let out a scream and the next thing she knew she was pitched into the wet snow. Behind her, the Doctor slammed the door and slid the bolt into position.

"Get away!" he shouted and raced off in the direction of the camp. With horror Sarah realized he still hoped to rescue Stevenson.

"There isn't time!" she cried, but the Doctor was already out of earshot. Sarah glanced again at the Power Unit. It was about to explode. She sprinted for the cover of the ridge.

Inside the Krynoid pounded the door in a frenzy. EIGHT . . . SEVEN . . . SIX . . . It managed to prise one tentacle through . . . FIVE . . . FOUR . . .

Sarah could see the ridge. Only a few yards further.

THREE . . . TWO . . .

The Doctor came in sight of the camp. He opened his mouth to yell. "Stev . . ." There was a searing flash of red, the ground shook, a firework seemed to explode in his head. Then he was sinking . . . sinking . . . sinking into a white cloud of nothingness . . .

5

Betrayal

Sarah woke. She found herself staring up at a clear blue sky. She tried to sit up but there was no sensation in her arms or legs. For one awful moment she wondered if she had lost them. Then she realized they were numb with cold.

Suddenly a foot crunched in the snow a few inches from her head. A muffled figure in furs and goggles loomed over her.

"I almost missed you in the snow," it said in a familiar English accent.

Sarah smiled weakly. "Yes, well, there's rather a lot of it about."

"Are you all right?"

"I think so."

The man helped her to her feet. "We're from South Bend. Medical Team. We heard the explosion. What happened?"

The explosion! It came back with a rush. The Doctor! Where was he? She began to run toward the camp like a mad thing. More figures jumped from a Snocat in pursuit. Panting, Sarah reached the top of the ridge only to let out a gasp of horror. Where once the camp had stood, there was now only a heap of blackened ash and twisted metal. A few wisps of smoke curled up into the blue sky. She looked back at the Power Unit. That too had completely disappeared.

Stunned, Sarah lowered her gaze. As she did so she gave a cry of fear. Sticking out of the snow a few feet away was a hand.

"Doctor!" she screamed, and began to clw frantically at the snow. Moments later strong arms arrived and pulled the inert figure of the Doctor from the snow. Desperately Sarah slapped his face to try and revive him. "Doctor! Wake up! *Wake Up*!"

For a while nothing happened. Then slowly one eye opened and winked. The grin she knew so well spread across the Doctor's face and he spoke. "Good morning."

Sarah breathed a sigh of relief and smiled back. She was never more grateful in her life to hear those two simple words.

Harrison Chase sat in his library glowing with triumph. On the desk in front of him stood the thermo-container.

"Well open it! Open it!" he ordered. Keeler removed the lid to reveal the pod. Chase stared at it with greedy fascination.

"I must hold it," he whispered and lovingly lifted out the strange, green object.

"It's all right in its present state," advised Keeler, "but we must be careful."

"Why?"

"The other pod infected one of their men."

Chase abruptly replaced the pod. "Infected? What happened?"

Keeler explained.

"Incredible!" said Chase. "You're sure the other one was destroyed?"

"The whole scientific base, and everybody in it, was obliterated," said Scorby smugly.

"Excellent. Regrettable, but excellent." Chase gazed at the pod once more. "Think of it, gentlemen," he said. "If the theory is correct, this has come to us across thousands of years and millions of miles."

"The last few miles caused a bit of trouble," muttered Scorby.

"Trouble?" scoffed Chase. "Nothing would be too much trouble for *this*!" The intercom buzzed on his desk. "Yes, Hargreaves?"

"Mr. Dunbar of WEB is here to see you, sir."

"Send him in." Chase clicked off the receiver.

A moment later, a distraught looking Dunbar was ushered in. He hesitated at the sight of Keeler and Scorby.

"It's all right," explained Chase smoothly. "These are the two men who brought back the pod."

Dunbar spoke with suppressed fury. "I had no idea you would go to such terrible lengths to get it!"

"The destruction of the others was necessary." Chase spoke without emotion.

"Necessary!" repeated Dunbar, appalled.

"You've been handsomely rewarded for your part, Dunbar, so put on a stiff upper lip and forget your qualms. The object has been achieved." Chase gestured toward the pod. "We can all relax."

Dunbar took a pace forward. "Not quite."

Chase stiffened. "What do you mean?"

"They weren't all wiped out. That's what I came to warn you about. The Doctor and his assistant are still alive."

"Impossible!" hissed Chase.

"The Doctor is meeting us at WEB in an hour's time." Dunbar waited for the effect of his news.

Keeler and Scorby shifted uneasily on the spot. Chase turned to face them, his eyes blazing. "You asinine bunglers!"

"You were very lucky, Doctor."

The speaker was Sir Colin Thackeray, Director of the World Ecology Bureau, a large distinguished-looking man with a rather precise manner.

"Simple presence of mind," replied the Doctor dismissively.

"Are you quite certain it was sabotage?" Dunbar spoke now.

"That explosion was no accident," said Sarah Jane firmly. She had recovered from the ordeal but appeared tired after the trip back to England.

Sir Colin looked puzzled. "Why on earth should anyone want to possess a thing like that so badly?"

"Greed! The most dangerous inpulse in the Galaxy," exclaimed the Doctor, jumping to his feet and addressing them all. "You realize that on this planet the pod is unique—I use the word with precision—and to some people its uniqueness makes it desirable at any cost."

"You make these men sound like fanatics," said Dunbar derisively.

The Doctor sauntered over to the side of the room and peered at a model of the Antarctic Base. "No," he said slowly, "I think they were working for someone else."

"The real fanatic," added Sarah.

"What's more to the point is how they got on to it." The Doctor spun around to face Dunbar. "The expedition had only reported its discovery to this office, right?"

Dunbar colored. "Doctor, I trust you aren't suggesting information was leaked from this Bureau?"

"Yes, what would be the gain from it?" intervened Sir Colin.

"Money," replied the Doctor sharply. "Thieves and murderers don't usually work for love."

"Since you seem to have this business sewn up, Doctor, where do you think the pod is now?" Dunbar sounded aggressive.

"I'd make a guess and say—right in this country." The Doctor crossed to Sir Colin and jabbed him in the chest. "Action, Sir Colin, that's what is needed. If we don't find that pod before it germinates, it will be the end of everything—even your pension!"

This last thought seemed to galvanize Sir Colin into activity. "Of course, Doctor, we'll do all we can to help. The entire facilities of this Bureau are at your disposal." He glared at his duputy, "All right, Dunbar?"

Dunbar nodded. "I'll organize anything you require."

"Good," snapped the Doctor. "Then organize us to the Botanical Institute."

A few minutes later the unmistakable figures of the Doctor and his assistant emerged from the entrance of the World Ecology Bureau. A uniformed chauffeur approached them. "Doctor?"

"Yes."

"This car was ordered for you, sir." He indicated a large, black limousine.

"How kind. After you, Sarah." They climbed in, the Doctor gave instructions to the chauffeur, and the car moved off.

Alone in his office, Dunbar dialed a number. Someone answered the other end. Dunbar leant closer into the phone and whispered, "It's all right, they're being taken care of."

"Excellent," replied the voice and hung up. Dunbar replaced the receiver thoughtfully.

The limousine was approaching the outskirts of London. The Doctor had remained pensive and silent throughout the journey and Sarah had chosen not to disturb him. She looked out of the window as the car turned down a side road and into open country. The Botanical Institute was farther out of town than she thought.

Suddenly the car lurched to a halt. The road had become little more than a dirt track leading to what seemed like a disused quarry. The Doctor jerked to life. "What's going on?"

The chauffeur turned around, a revolver in his hand. "We're in a nice deserted place, Doctor. Now—both of you—out!" He slipped from behind the wheel and, keeping them covered, opened the rear passenger door.

The Doctor winked. "I think we'd better do as he says, Sarah." He started to get out slowly. Then, in one explosive action he swung the door violently at the chauffeur, knocked him flying into the mud and dragged Sarah from the car.

"Run!" he yelled, and the two of them sprinted away down the rutted track. Winded, the chauffeur groped for his revolver, but before he could take aim the two figures disappeared down a gully. He staggered to his feet and set off in pursuit.

One quick glance was sufficient for the Doctor to take in the quarry. A large sandhopper with a raised platform lay to their right. He changed direction toward it, shouting instructions to Sarah as he did so.

A few moments later the panting gunman arrived beneath the hopper. His captives had vanished—into thin air! To his left was an old pile of gravel, enough for a hiding place. He crept toward it, finger on the trigger. Suddenly, there was a noise behind him. He spun around and fired.

Twenty feet above his head the Doctor crouched on the hopper platform, poised to leap. He could see Sarah plainly behind the gravel pile. She picked up a second pebble and threw it in the air. The chauffeur turned and fired again, then took a pace forward, bringing him directly below the Doctor.

The Doctor eyed the drop one more time, noted the position of the revolver and launched himself into space. Thud! The chauffeur crumpled like a rag doll as the Doctor's two hundred and seventeen pounds slammed into him. Sarah dashed out from behind the mound. The Doctor picked himself up and was about to administer a straight left when he realized his dive had laid the gunman out cold.

"He isn't dead?" said Sarah fearfully.

"Unconscious. It seems news travels fast from the South Pole."

The Doctor gathered up the revolver and hurled it out of sight. "Let's search the car."

They ran back.

Clearly the limousine did not belong to the World Ecology Bureau. But who did own it? There appeared to be no clues inside the car.

Sarah suddenly called the Doctor to the trunk. She was holding up a framed painting of a flower. In the corner was a signature.

"Amelia Ducat," read the Doctor, puzzled.

"An original as well," exclaimed Sarah excitedly. "Must be worth something."

"You think so?"

Sarah eyed the Doctor with disdain. "You mean to say you haven't heard of Amelia Ducat? She's one of the country's leading flower artists."

The Doctor glanced in the direction of the sandhopper. "Hardly a passion for a gunman," he said with a grin. "Still, let's see if Miss Ducat can throw any light on the subject."

He leapt into the driving seat and, scarcely allowing Sarah time to climb in, accelerated off toward the main road.

"Ah yes . . . perfect example of *Fritillaria Meleagris.*"

The speaker was an eccentric little lady in her sixties, dressed in heavy tweeds; a pair of gold-rimmed spectacles dangled on a chain around her neck and a large cigar jutted from the side of her mouth. She held the painting at arm's length admiringly. "Rather good, don't you think?"

The Doctor smiled indulgently. "We're trying to trace the owner, Miss Ducat."

"You mean it isn't yours?"

"No. We found it in a car truck."

"In a car trunk?" Miss Ducat looked horrified. "How insensitive!"

"So was the driver," chipped in Sarah. "He tried to kill us."

"Good gracious! Whatever for?"

The Doctor leant over the top of Miss Ducat's easel, which held a half-completed painting. "Miss Ducat," he said, in his friendliest and most coaxing tone, "do you remember who bought this painting?"

Miss Ducat stared, a little puzzled, at the painting in front of her. "Nobody. It isn't finished yet."

"No, this one, Miss Ducat," explained Sarah. "*Fritillaria* Melewhatsit."

"Ah . . . oh . . . let me see now . . ." Miss Ducat took a couple of good puffs on her cigar and coughed violently. "It was six or seven years ago . . ." She closed her eyes in deep concentration. "Lace? . . . Mace? . . . Paice? . . . Race? . . ." Miss Ducat struggled manfully.

"Brace?" said Sarah.

"Grace?" tried the Doctor.

"Chase!" shouted Miss Ducat triumphantly. "Harrison Chase the millionaire!" A strange look came over her. "Good Lord," she said. "He never paid me!"

Sarah glanced at the Doctor who suppressed a smile. "Give me his address, Miss Ducat," he said, "and I'll see what I can do."

Twenty minutes later the large, black limousine was crusing effortlessly through the countryside, the Doctor at the wheel. He was dressed in the chauffeur's dark blue raincoat.

"I hope this works," said Sarah doubtfully.

"A risk worth taking," replied the Doctor seriously. "We must find that pod."

The road now ran alongside the high wall of an estate, topped with barbed wire, and signs at intervals marked "DANGER—KEEP OUT."

The Doctor spotted the gateway ahead and pulled the car into the verge. "Ready?" He smiled encouragingly at Sarah. She ducked down beneath the windshield out of sight. The Doctor doffed the chauffeur's peaked cap, glanced appreciatively at himself in the mirror and eased the car forward.

The heavy wooden gates were at least twenty feet high and studded with metal bolts like a prison entrance. From the look of things Mr. Harrison Chase was a gentleman who valued his privacy. He was also a gentleman with friends in high places. On past evidence, their little *contretemps* with the chauffeur would soon be reported, and before then the Doctor knew he had to somehow penetrate Chase's domain and retrieve the pod.

He swung the car in front of the gates and beeped the horn. A uniformed guard poked his head through a small door set in the right-hand gate. He glanced at the car, nodded, then disappeared inside. Seconds later the gates parted and the Doctor accelerated through. The guard stood back as the car swept past, hardly giving it a look, then shut the gates again. The Doctor breathed a sigh of relief. He had banked correctly on this being a routine procedure.

They were now in the grounds of a large and imposing manor house, glimpses of which the Doctor caught through thick greenery bordering the approach road. He slowed down, searching for a fork which would lead around to the back of the property. Sure enough there was one. He steered the big car expertly down a narrow drive and pulled to a halt beneath a clump of trees.

"So far so good," he whispered, and tapped Sarah on the shoulder.

She straightened up from her hiding position. "Ouch! I'm sure there are more comfortable ways of traveling." She rubbed her back painfully.

"We'll leave the car here," said the Doctor, ignoring her complaint. He switched off the ignition and slid gently out of the car. Sarah did likewise.

The nearest place of cover was a crumbling wall

with a series of elegant arches set into it. The Doctor moved silently toward the wall, Sarah in tow. From there they could see the house clearly across a wild expanse of overgrown lawn.

It was a magnificent Elizabethan manor house, large and rambling, with several courtyards and outbuildings running off it. The gardens immediately surrounding the house were a blaze of color, a breathtaking profusion of flowers of every kind, but further from the house the vegetation grew thicker and more exotic, forming a jungle-like screen around the whole property.

"Lovely house," whispered Sarah. "What's the best way in?"

"Not the front door, I'm afraid."

At that moment two uniformed guards appeared. The were no more than fifty yards away. Over their shoulders they carried vicious looking sten guns. It was obvious their course would bring them straight to where the Doctor and Sarah were hiding.

"We'll have to bluff it," whispered the Doctor and stepped nonchalantly out into the open. Sarah's heart skipped a beat as she followed suit. Any second she expected to be enveloped in a hail of bullets. At the same time she found herself laughing inwardly at the comical figure of the Doctor, in the chauffeur's hat and coat, attempting to walk quickly yet casually away from the guards.

They were half way toward the house when a voice rang out behind them. "Hey you!" The Doctor quickened his pace. "Halt!" The sound of a safety catch being released was clearly audible.

"Run!" yelled the Doctor as he sprinted toward a narrow gate at the side of the house.

"I said halt!"

The Doctor burst open the gate with his shoulder and pushed Sarah through. As he did so a shower of bullets slammed into the masonry inches above his head and alarm bells began to ring inside the house.

They were now running along a narrow terrace. Suddenly, more guards appeared at the far end. The Doctor grabbed Sarah's arm and leapt with her off the terrace onto the ground and headed on a zigzag course toward the surrounding cover of trees. The barking of tracker dogs could be heard above the din of bells and machine-gun fire. "One thing is certain," thought the Doctor, "Harrison Chase doesn't take kindly to strangers."

Seconds later they reached the belt of trees and plunged in. Branches, thorns and razor-sharp leaves cut their skin and clawed at their clothing as they crashed through the jungle-like vegetation.

"This way, Sarah," gasped the Doctor and struck out to his left. The hue and cry was falling behind them and to their right. Any plan to penetrate the house was now useless, but if they could make the outer wall, thought the Doctor, they might still escape. Ahead of them appeared a solid mass of giant bamboo. Sarah felt she was acting out a nightmare. This couldn't be happening in England. The Doctor beat a way through. "Come on, nearly there!" Sarah willed herself on.

Suddenly, she literally fell into a clearing. Ahead was a small pathway. The Doctor saw her fall and ran back. "Quick!" He hauled her to her feet and dragged her forward again. The blood was pounding through her veins and her lungs were bursting for air. Then, all at once, Sarah felt the Doctor's grip slacken. He had stopped.

"Hello, Doctor, I heard you were on your way."

Sarah froze as the unmistakable voice of Scorby cut through the air. Gun in hand, his familiar dark figure blocked the pathway ahead. At the same moment three armed guards appeared from nowhere and seized them both.

Scorby stepped up to them, savoring the moment. "You weren't thinking of leaving, I hope. Mr. Chase is so looking forward to meeting you."

6

A Visit to Harrison Chase

Moments later the Doctor and Sarah found themselves inside the house. They were bundled along dark corridors and through a doorway into a large baronial hall. An oak-beamed ceiling towered above their heads, and on either side the paneled walls were lined with suits of armor and ancient hanging tapestries.

At the far end, seated in a throne-like chair, sat an immaculately dressed man wearing black gloves. Not for the first time in his life the Doctor sensed he was in the presence of danger and evil.

The figure rose as the two captives were pushed forward. "So, the meddling Doctor." The Doctor felt the man's powerful gaze sweep over him. "You lead a charmed life. Not even a touch of frostbite."

The Doctor eyes his opponent with undisguised contempt. "Are you behind this whole murderous exercise?"

Ignoring the Doctor's challenge the man turned to Sarah. "And Miss Smith—still beautifully intact, I see." He leered at her.

"No thanks to your friend over there," retorted Sarah, indicating Scorby.

"Hand over the pod, Chase," commanded the

Doctor in a voice of steel. "You're tampering with things you don't understand."

Chase gave a chuckle. "Hand it over? After all the trouble I've taken to acquire it? No, Doctor. My pod, when it finally flowers, will be the crowning glory of a life's work." The voice grew shrill and excited. "Perhaps you didn't know, Doctor, that I have assembled in this house the greatest collection of rare plants in the world."

"Yes, I've noticed a bit of greenfly here and there."

Chase's expression turned sour. "Your envy, Doctor, is understandable. However, since I propose to have you both executed . . ."

Sarah gasped incredulously. "You're not going to kill us?"

"My dear Miss Smith, you leave me no option." The voice regained its smooth, feline purr. "You and the Doctor keep interfering . . . As I was saying, however, you will be granted a unique privilege before you die."

"How generous," remarked the Doctor with heavy sarcasm.

Chase smiled coldly. "The last thing you will ever see will be my beautiful collection of plants. Come this way." He crossed to a side door.

"I've heard of flower power but this is ridiculous," muttered Sarah under her breath.

A dig in the ribs from Scorby's gun put an end to further conversation, and she and the Doctor were propelled out of the room.

They were led to another part of the house, into what looked like a large laboratory. Various experiments seemed to be in progress, supervised by white-coated technicians. Plants were being nourished by drips, like hospital patients, or supported on strange metal structures suspended from the ceiling. Chase ushered them in with mock politeness and pointed to a flower the Doctor had never seen before. "This is the famous Shanghai Saffron. It . . . er . . . defected from the East last spring."

The Doctor remained unimpressed. "Are we going much further?" he said. "I do so hate guided tours."

Chase moved on, unheeding. "Here we treat our green friends as patients. If they are puny, we build them up; if they are sick, we give them succor." He paused by a row of plants which faced a battery of flashing blue bulbs.

"These must feel they're in a disco," quipped Sarah.

Chase smiled. "You've heard of the theory that irregular light patterns can affect the senses of so-called mindless things?"

The Doctor nodded. "Yes, like Scorby here. Incidentally, where's his friend?"

"Keeler is engaged in important isolated research."

"On the pod?"

"But of course."

They continued toward a pair of large metallic doors, engraved with swirling designs in the shape of flowers. Chase swung them open with a flourish.

The sight which met their eyes made Sarah gasp with astonishment and even the Doctor raised an eyebrow in surprise. Before them lay a vast expanse of luxuriant foliage. It spread out in all directions so that it was impossible to tell where the forest of green ended and the walls and ceiling began. As his two prisoners eyed the vivid tangle of plants and creepers, Chase strode to a gleaming metal box set into the stone wall and fiddled with some knobs. Immediately the air was filled with an eerie, discordant sound.

"The song of the plants," cried Chase. "I composed it myself. People say you should talk to plants. I believe that, just as I believe they also like music."

"Doctor, we must get out of here," whispered Sarah in desperation.

"Yes, the music is terrible." The Doctor grinned at her. Sarah grimaced. This was no time for jokes. She scanned the room for possible exits, but apart from a long iron cat-walk which led into the thick of the creepers, there was nothing.

Suddenly an agitated figure, obviously the butler, burst into the room behind them. "Mr. Chase!" he called.

The music stopped abruptly. "What is it, Hargreaves?"

"It's Mr. Keeler—something is happening to that thing, sir. He wants you to go to the Special Projects room straight away."

burst into the room behind them. "Mr. Chase!" he
pointed at the Doctor and Sarah. "I'll join you in a moment. I'm sure our two friends won't mind a slight delay before they die." He swept toward the door.

The Doctor shouted after him. "You're insane, Chase! You don't know what a terrible thing you are unleashing!"

Chase gave a sinister smile, but said nothing. An instant later he was gone.

Scorby immediately took command. He dismissed the remaining guards, then propelled the Doctor and Sarah out of the room at gunpoint. As they passed through seemingly endless stone corridors, the Doctor reflected dismally on their plight.

They had fallen into the clutches of a madman—without doubt—and despite warnings, he was evidently conducting his own experiments on the pod. It was imperative to get to the pod and prevent any further risk. But how? They were being led to their deaths this very instant.

By now they had left the house and were being marched through the overgrown gardens. "Where are you taking us, Scorby?" asked the Doctor.

"Don't worry, it's strictly a one-way journey," came the chilling reply.

Ahead lay the same arched wall which had concealed them less than an hour beforehand. Imperceptibly the Doctor quickened his pace. Sarah was a fraction behind and a little to his right. Scorby followed, covering them with his gun.

As he drew level with the nearest arch the Doctor took a sudden step to his left, thus putting solid masonry between himself and the gun. Taken unawares Scorby let out a cry and raised his arm to fire. But the fleeting figure of the Doctor dodged about the arches without presenting a clear target. In the split second that Scorby's attention was diverted, Sarah seized her chance and leapt on his arm like a tigress. As Scorby struggled to shake himself free, the Doctor darted in and sent the gun flying with a skilled, mule-like kick. Scorby wrenched himself clear of Sarah and lunged at the Doctor. The Doctor side-stepped, grabbed his head in a Venusian neck lock, and gave it a short, sharp twist. There was a nasty click and Scorby sank to the ground.

"Time to leave," said the Doctor calmly, but Sarah needed no bidding this time, and the two of them hared off toward the undergrowth.

Once they had gained cover the Doctor paused.

"We can't handle this on our own," he said. "Sir Colin must be warned about the danger."

"Right, so let's get out and phone him," responded Sarah urgently.

"*You* are going to phone him," ordered the Doctor. "I'm staying here."

Sarah began to argue but the Doctor cut her off. "I must get a look at that pod . . . see what state it's in." He tore off the chauffeur's clothes. "Come on, the outer wall can't be far."

Pistol shots could now be heard and the distant barking of guard dogs. The Doctor led Sarah stealthily through the undergrowth like an Indian brave until, finally, they reached the high wall which skirted the perimeter of the grounds. Luckily the barbed wire had come away in places and there was just enough room for Sarah to squeeze through.

"Fancy a little mountaineering?" said the Doctor and hoisted Sarah onto his shoulders. The gun shots and barking were growing nearer. With difficulty, Sarah heaved herself to the top of the wall. There was a fifteen-foot drop on the other side.

"All right?" whispered the Doctor.

"I think so." She took a deep breath and let go.

The Doctor heard her land heavily. "The main road should be straight ahead. Good luck."

"And to you."

The Doctor waited until he was sure Sarah was on her way, then quickly retraced his steps toward the house.

Sarah pressed on toward the main road. She could hear the odd car passing and this kept her on a straight course. Although she was out of the grounds there was still a large stretch of woodland between herself and safety.

Suddenly, she froze like a statue. A twig had snapped nearby. In front of her was a dense thicket. She scanned every branch and leaf for sign of movement. There was another, fluttering sound, then a blackbird flew out of a bush. Sarah let go her breath with relief and continued forward.

The next thing she knew a large hairy hand was clamped over her mouth and a voice from behind said, "Make a sound, little girl, and you're dead."

In the Special Projects room Chase was crouched inches away from the pod, as if in a trance. "It's growing! It's alive!" he murmured, his eyes wide with rapture.

"I shouldn't get too close," warned Keller. "From what happened at the camp base, the germination could be spontaneous. It's alien, don't forget."

Chase continued to stare spellbound at the pod. It was larger now, more bloated looking, and several cracks had begun to appear on the surface.

Suddenly Chase snapped out of his reverie. "Inject more fixed nitrogen!" he ordered.

Keeler hesitated. "I don't think that would be wise."

Chase glared at him. "I pay you, Keeler, so that *I* can make the decisions. Now, inject another fifteen grams!"

Keeler nodded nervously and carried out the order.

The Doctor halted and peered through a clump of bushes toward the house. So far so good. He had performed a detour and calculated correctly that it would bring him out at the rear of the building. Apart from one guard posted on a corner he had a free run to some stone steps leading down to a basement door. Once in the house he then had to find the Special Projects room. He had a hunch it might be on the top floor where there would be plenty of light and more privacy.

He waited. The guard was still facing toward him. After a few moments the guard took out a walkie-talkie receiver and put it to his ear. From his reaction the Doctor guessed he was receiving orders, perhaps news of their escape. The guard pocketed the receiver, took a quick glance around then ran off down the side of the house. The Doctor seized his opportunity and belted toward the steps. The door opened easily and he entered.

He was in a long, dark passage with a flag-stone floor. At the far end was a narrow staircase, originally for the servants' use, but probably still a good route to the top of the house. Cautiously, he traversed the passage and started up the stairs.

"I don't like it. It's like waiting for a bomb to explode." Keeler rubbed his hands together in agitation and paced the room.

"Where's your enthusiasm, Keeler?" crowed Chase gleefully. "This promises to be the high point of your career—a moment of history!"

Chase's triumphant mood was abruptly shattered as Scorby burst in, dragging Sarah behind him.

"I thought you had them safely locked up?" he hissed.

They escaped," replied Scorby sheepishly. "A guard found this one in the woods beyond the wall. The Doctor's still at large."

Chase crossed to Sarah and grabbed her savagely beneath the chin. "Where is he?" he demanded.

Sarah stared defiantly back at him. "I don't know, and if I did I wouldn't tell you."

"How uncooperative. However, I've just had an idea. You're going to help with my experiment. Remove her coat."

Scorby quickly tore Sarah's coat from her shoulders. "What are we going to do, boss?"

Chase dragged Sarah over to the bench. "Miss Smith will be our subject . . . like so. Get some clamps!" He forced Sarah's arm on to the bench. Sarah let out a gasp of horror as she caught sight of the pod.

"You can't! It's inhuman!" protested Keeler.

"I don't care," cried Chase. "I must see what happens when the Krynoid touches human flesh!"

Sarah struggled desperately as they clamped her arm to the bench. Already the pod was beginning to throb and split in places. Chase stood gloating at the sight, like a fiend possessed.

The Doctor reached the top of the stairs. It was dark and dusty, and there was very little headroom. Through the gloom he could just make out a door down a narrow passage. He clambered along and tried the knob. The door opened to reveal an attic with a second door which led onto the roof of the house. He crawled out. To his left was a large section made of glass. He edged toward it and peered through.

The sight which met him made his blood run cold. Twenty feet below in the room, Sarah was imprisoned in a chair, with one arm clamped to a wooden bench. Less than twelve inches away lay the pod, hideously swollen and vibrating menacingly. Even as the Doctor looked it began to break open.

7

Condemned to Die

The Doctor launched himself through the glass roof in a spectacular dive, landing feet first on the bench. It snapped instantly beneath his weight, spewing plants, instruments and broken glass in all directions. Before anyone had time to react, the Doctor hurled Scorby to the ground, grabbed his gun and yanked Sarah clear of the pod.

"Untie her!" he yelled fiercely. Keeler started to release Sarah.

Chase, his hands held high, watched in cool amusement. "What do you do for an encore, Doctor?" he asked.

The Doctor leveled the gun at Chase. "I win," he smiled. "Come on, Sarah."

Sarah followed the Doctor to the door. He pushed her outside, followed then quickly slammed the door and locked it behind them.

Chase ran across the room and hammered on the door in impotent fury. "Guards! Guards!"

Stunned by the force of the Doctor's throw, Scorby stirred and groaned feebly. Chase continued to pound the door.

Suddenly, a blood-curdling scream rent the air. "Aaarrgh! . . . my arm . . . my arm . . ."

Chase spun around. In the midst of the confusion the pod had burst, and now a long green tendril was digging into the flesh of Keeler's right arm. A look of horrified fascination came over Chase as Keeler began to stagger around the room in agony. An instant later, the door was thrown open and a mob of guards rushed in.

"Quick! Get after the Doctor and that girl," ordered Chase. "They must not escape!"

The guards charged off. Chase went back to Keeler. Already a terrifying change was taking place. Keeler's face and arms were turning a strange, mottled green.

"Do something . . ." he pleaded, overcome with shock and fear.

Chase watched in icy detachment. "Amazing . . . absolutely unique!"

"What's happening?" Scorby came around muzzily, then let out a cry of disbelief as he focused on Keeler.

"Slept well, did you?" snarled Chase. "Now get out and find that Doctor!" Scorby picked himself off the floor and hurried out. "And be careful, he's got your gun!" Chase yelled after him. He turned to Keeler. "We've got to get over to the cottage, where we can look after you properly."

There was something in the way Chase said this which made Keeler's blood run cold, but before he had time to protest he was being manhandled out of the room by his master and the ever present Hargreaves.

After escaping, the Doctor led Sarah down the rear stairs and out of the house. He had noticed earlier a small shed set against a stone wall, used for storing garden equipment. He hurriedly guided Sarah toward it and thrust her in.

"Keep out of sight. I'll be back as soon as I can."

"Where are you going?"

"To destroy the pod . . . before it's too late."

Sarah looked horrified. "You can't tackle them single-handed."

The Doctor flourished Scorby's pistol. "I've got a gun."

"You'd never use it."

The Doctor grinned. "True. But they don't know that." He gave her a reassuring squeeze and crept off. Sarah climbed into her hidey hole, and settled down to wait.

Hidden by the thick foliage, the Doctor watched the rear of the building as a group of heavy-booted guards emerged and fanned out into the grounds. Then, when all was clear, he flitted across to the basement door and re-entered the house. Using the same route as before he quickly reached the entrance to the Special Projects room. The door was ajar and no sound came from within. Puzzled, the Doctor tiptoed in, gun at the ready.

The room was empty. With a pang of dismay the Doctor saw the pod had already burst open. He crossed the debris-strewn floor and, laying his gun aside, picked up a fragment of the pod to examine it.

"Rather stupid of you to return, Doctor," said an unpleasant voice from the doorway.

The Doctor spun around to see Scorby covering him with a machine gun. "I see I am too late. The pod has burst. I hope there was no one in the way."

"Unfortunately there was. Our friend Keeler. Very clumsy of him."

"Then we could all be doomed," said the Doctor quietly.

"Don't exaggerate, Doctor," snarled Scorby. "Where's the girl?"

"Gone to get help," lied the Doctor. Then, with vehemence, "You're working for a madman, Scorby, you know that?"

"He pays well," came the reply. "And don't lie about Miss Smith. She'll never get out of this place . . . alive." He pocketed the pistol on the bench and motioned the Doctor out of the room.

The two of them marched quickly along a series of corridors and stairways toward the other end of the house.

"Not another guided tour, I hope," quipped the Doctor.

"You'll soon see this is no time for joking," replied Scorby, stopping at a gray, metal door. He opened it and pushed the Doctor in. "Mr. Chase has prepared a highly novel method for your execution."

The Doctor descended a flight of stone steps and found himself in a large basement room filled with dustbins and refuse. At the far end stood a huge piece of machinery, covering one entire wall. It consisted of two enormous metal rollers with steel blades, like a giant lawn mower. The rollers were fed by a wide aluminum conveynor belt with vertical polished sides, about six feet deep. The Doctor guessed there must be a chute behind the rollers which led out through the wall and into the gardens.

The front of the conveyor belt was lowered at the moment, like a drawbridge, and a guard was busy empting waste into it. The guard stopped work as they entered and, at Scorby's command, proceeded to bind the Doctor's arms and legs with a length of thick rope.

The Doctor eyed Scorby's machine gun and realized there was little point in resisting. He inspected his surroundings nonchalantly and sniffed the air. "Isn't it about time you emptied the rubbishbins?"

"We will," said Scorby. "Soon," and he gave a peculiar smile.

Sarah looked anxiously at her watch. The Doctor had been gone almost an hour. That could only mean one thing.

She peered out. Dusk had already fallen and it was probably dark enough to afford some cover. Sarah made her decision. She had to act now, either to escape and get help or rescue the Doctor herself. *If* she could find him. She emerged warily from hiding and moved off.

Unknown to Sarah, but not far away, Chase and Hargreaves had dragged the infected Keeler to a cottage in the grounds. He now lay upstairs on a bed staring vacantly at the ceiling, while the butler pinioned his arms and legs with strong rope.

The activity seemed to shake him out of his stupor and he suddenly began to struggle. "What are you doing?"

"It's for your own good," said Chase.

"You can't keep me here. I need proper medical attention." He tried to move an arm but fell back exhausted. His skin was rapidly changing into a vegetable texture and his limbs were beginning to lose their human shape.

"Remarkable," said Chase excitedly. "We must observe the process carefully."

Keeler looked pleadingly at Hargreaves. "Don't

listen to him. This isn't an experiment—it's murder!"

"You're privileged, Keeler," continued Chase enraptured. "You're becoming a plant . . . a marvellous new species of plant!"

He rose and beckoned Hargreaves to the door. "Don't worry," he whispered, "everything will be all right, just so long as we keep him here." He led the butler out of the bedroom and down the stairs.

Sarah hurried through the undergrowth. It was now dark and difficult to see. She suspected she was lost and a feeling of panic began to grip her.

Suddenly she came to a path. Voices sounded ahead and a flicker of light illuminated the grass. Straining her eyes she made out a small, thatched cottage. As she watched, the low wooden door opened and Chase and the butler stepped out. They walked briskly along the path toward her. Sarah darted back into the shadows. The two men brushed past without noticing her and disappeared into the gloom.

For a second she was tempted to follow, but intuition told her to investigate the cottage. It was just possible the Doctor had been taken there as prisoner. She crept forward and gently opened the door.

Inside, the cottage was dark, apart from a glimmer of candlelight overhead. Sarah groped her way to the foot of the stairs. All at once she heard a sound, a pitiful inhuman moan, which chilled her spine. Shaking, she mounted the steps. At the top stood a closed wooden door. She raised the latch and entered.

The sight in the room transfixed her with horror. A monstrous, hybrid creature lay on the bed, half human, half vegetable.

"You should be glad," it croaked. "This might have been you."

Sarah could not speak as the hideous picture swam before her eyes.

"This must be how Winlett changed," continued the voice. "You saw him at the base, didn't you?"

Sarah nodded.

"What was he like? You've got to tell me."

Sarah forced herself to look at the grotesque shape on the bed. It was true. The process was happening all over again. And she was powerless to stop it.

"Why are they keeping you here?" she managed to whisper finally.

"Chase . . . Chase owns me, body and soul."

"I must get to the Doctor," said Sarah urgently.

A cunning expression appeared on the creature's face. "Let me loose," it breathed. "We'll go together." It strained at the ropes.

Sarah hesitated. She could no longer be sure. "You aren't well enough," she said, trying to conceal her fear.

"You're as bad as Chase and the others!" The voice became hard and rasping.

"That's not true."

". . . You want me to die?" The figure struggled to rise.

Alarmed, Sarah backed toward the door. As she did so she heard a noise from below. Someone was entering the cottage! She looked around frantically for somewhere to hide as heavy footsteps ascended the stairs.

8

The Krynoid Strikes

The footsteps halted outside the door. Just in time Sarah spied a large wardrobe standing in a corner. She snatched it open and dived in.

Through a narrow chink in the wardrobe she watched as the black-jacketed figure of Hargreaves entered the room. He carried a silver tray which he placed beside the bed. The creature had slumped back as if semi-conscious, and lay quietly groaning. On the tray were chunks of raw meat. The butler made sure the food was within reach of the creature's "arm," then after checking the ropes were still secure, he left the room.

As soon as she heard the front door close, Sarah emerged from the wardrobe. She gave a final, horrified glance at the bed, and slipped quietly away.

Once out of the cottage Sarah tried to get her bearings. It was very dark, although a little pale moonlight filtered down through the trees, casting spooky shadows. Sarah shivered. It was only a matter of time now before the creature in the cottage became a second, deadly Krynoid. The Doctor had to be warned, always supposing he was still alive. Sarah quickly banished that awful thought from her mind and set off through the trees. If the Doctor were captive he must be in the house, and the house could not be far away because Hargreaves had returned so soon with the food.

She followed a narrow winding footpath which crossed a stream by a small footbridge. Sure enough there was the main house, about two hundred yards beyond. One or two lights shone out on to the surrounding gardens and she could see uniformed guards patrolling the ground floor.

Soundlessly, Sarah tiptoed across the thick grass and gained the cover of the outside wall. Then she worked her way methodically around the house until she came to some steps leading down to a basement door. Without knowing it, she had stumbled on the same entrance as the Doctor. She slid into the dark stone corridor and made her way stealthily toward the interior of the house.

The Doctor glanced uneasily at the crushing machine for the umpteenth time. He was now in no doubt about his imminent execution or the manner in which it would take place. Every ten minutes he had been privileged to witness the giant rollers of the machine devour several tons of garbage in no uncertain fashion. It was clear that the addition of one extra, live body would not cause the slightest hiccup in the functioning of this engineering masterpiece.

These morbid reflections were brought to an abrupt halt as the ever watchful guard sprang to attention. A moment later Harrison Chase entered.

He smiled grimly at the Doctor. "You've seen my little toy?"

"Most efficient," demurred the Doctor.

"The problem is keeping it stocked up." Chase gestured toward the empty bins.

"Yes. At the moment it's working on an empty stomach," joked the Doctor wryly. As if to emphasize this point the machine shuddered to a stop.

Chase crossed to the wall and reset the timer. "The next time," he purred, "we must give it something to chew on." He looked meaningfully at the Doctor. "You may have noticed how lush the grounds are. This is the secret." He patted the side of the crusher affectionately. "We use everything in the grinder . . . every scrap of food and gardening waste . . . lots of other things too . . . provided they are organic."

The Doctor at that moment felt decidedly organic. "What's happening to Keeler?" he asked, changing the subject.

"None of us can help Keeler now," came the smooth reply, "but properly nurtured he can be of inestimable value to science."

With a shock the Doctor realized Keeler had become another of Chase's experiments. Was there no end to this man's devilry? He fixed Chase with an iron stare. "Don't you understand what you are breeding?"

"A plant, Doctor, a human plant. And nothing is going to stop me." Chase motioned to the guard who prodded the Doctor on to the aluminium conveyor belt and clossed off the access door. Hands and feet tied, he was now crouched in the belly of the crusher, the vertical metal sides giving him no hope of escape and effectively screening out his vision. In front, a few feet away, hung the lethal steel blades, motionless for the time being.

He heard Chase turn a switch on the wall. "Your death, Doctor, will be agonizing, but mercifully quick."

"How considerate."

"After shredding," intoned Chase's voice, "your remains will pass automatically through my Compost Acceleration Chamber, and within ten minutes you will be pumped into the garden to become part of nature's grand design."

"But the Krynoid isn't part of that design, Chase," retorted the Doctor. "Once its growth starts, you'll never manage to contain it. Nobody will be safe!"

Chase let out a loud cackle. "You underestimate me, Doctor. Now say your prayers. You have only a few minutes left." The hideous laugh rang out again. Then the door was slammed shut and everything went quiet, except for the faint ticking of the automatic time switch.

On the main road a few hundred yards from the entrance to Chase's estate, a dark gray Rover three liter was parked surreptitiously under the trees, its lights doused. Inside sat Sir Colin Thackeray and Dunbar.

"I don't like it," said Sir Colin grimly. "I don't like it at all." He drummed his fingers on the steering wheel.

Dunbar remained silent. He seemed distracted, as if wrestling with something inside himself.

"I'm going to call in the Doctor's friends at UNIT," snapped Sir Colin finally. "This is getting too big for us."

"No, wait!" interrupted Dunbar. "Let me go in alone."

"You'll never get past the gate."

"Yes I will," replied Dunbar quietly.

"What?"

"I've made a terrible mistake, Sir Colin. It's my duty now to try and save the situation."

Before Sir Colin could stop him, Dunbar sprang out of the car. "Give me half an hour. If I'm not back by then, return to London and contact UNIT." He slammed the car door shut and hurried off into the darkness.

Sarah paused. The house was a rabbit-warren of corridors and passageways, any one of which could lead straight into the arms of the guards. Her progress so far had been slow and cautious.

Suddenly she heard a strange noise—a kind of grinding and thumping. It seemed to be coming from under the floor! She looked around. There was a small door at the far end of the passage. She opened it and found a flight of stone steps leading down to a lower level. The noise grew louder. She crept along this underground passage until she was directly beneath the spot where she had first heard the sound. A heavy metal door, not immediately visible, was recessed into the stone wall. The thumping noise came from inside.

Swiftly, Sarah heaved the door open. Straightaway her ears were split by a deafening blast of sound, as if huge strips of metal were being ripped apart and pounded into pieces. This thunderous screeching emanated from a mass of moving machinery at the far end of the room. Two enormous rollers were rising and falling in unison, slowly grinding together as they did so like a pair of giant molars. In front, a shiny aluminium conveyor belt was chugging inexorably toward this gaping maw. In it lay the Doctor!

Sarah flew across the room. "Doctor!"

"Quick, Sarah, the switch!" he yelled above the din. His head was only inches from the murderous whirling blades.

Desperately Sarah scanned the wall. There were several levers. She pulled one. The noise increased and the machinery began to accelerate.

"The other one!" cried the Doctor.

Sarah yanked a second lever. Nothing happened. The Doctor was flattened against the sides of the conveyor. The rollers reared up again and began to descend toward him. In a mad flurry Sarah pulled all the levers she could find. Suddenly the noise subsided, the rollers ceased their descent, and came to rest a hair's breadth from the Doctor's face. Sarah let out a sob of relief and ran to release him. The Doctor looked up and gave her a charming smile.

"I believe that's what's known as a close shave," he said.

Pale and tense, Dunbar confronted Chase across the wide baronial hall.

"Abandon the experiment? My dear Dunbar, nothing will stop me now. This is the most valuable study in plant biology ever made." The ghost of a smile flickered over his cat-like features.

Suddenly a distraught-looking Hargreaves rushed in.

"What is it?" snapped Chase, annoyed by this unusual interruption.

"That thing in the cottage . . . it's breaking loose!"

Chase's jaw dropped. "It can't be . . ."

"The ropes, sir. They're not going to hold it!"

"You mean that monster could be roaming around?" cut in Dunbar.

"I'm afraid so, sir."

Dunbar's eyes widened in alarm at the thought.

All at once, there was a scuffle of footsteps and

Scorby burst into the room. "The Doctor's escaped!"

"He seems to be making a habit of it!" said Chase, his face contorting into a paroxysm of rage.

Dunbar took a pace forward and gripped the desk. "You're mad, Chase! Raving mad!" He was beginning to sweat.

"There's no need to panic, Dunbar."

"I'm going to get help. If this thing is free it could kill us all!" He started to back toward the door.

Chase's voice, icy cold, stabbed the air. "I would prefer it if nobody else was told of this, Dunbar."

"No. It's all gone far enough. I'm getting out of here and no one's going to stop me." Dunbar suddenly drew a gun and brandished it hysterically.

"You won't make it past the guards," said Chase coolly.

Dunbar reached the open doorway. "We'll see."

Scorby reached for his own gun but before he could use it Dunbar let off a shot. The men in the room ducked instinctively, giving Dunbar time to slam the door and belt off down the corridor.

While this was happening Sarah had swiftly and expertly guided the Doctor back to the cottage. Now, as they approached the low thatched building, Sarah started to tremble. The Doctor drew closer and gave her hand a reassuring squeeze.

They entered and climbed the stairs. Everything was ominously quiet. The Doctor carefully eased open the bedroom door and peered in.

The bed was empty. The ropes lay shattered, burst like string by a superhuman force.

"Where's it gone?" whispered Sarah.

The Doctor gave her a grim look. There was only

one place the Krynoid could be; lurking in the blackness outside, just as its predecessor had prowled the snowy wastes several days before.

There was no time to lose! The Doctor leapt down the rickety wooden steps, grabbed a rusty sword from above the fireplace and dashed out into the night with Sarah in tow.

Dunbar moved through the woods, pistol at the ready. The most he had gained was a minute's start. Scorby and the guards, with machine guns and dogs, were already tracking him down. Escape through the main gate was impossible. He had to give them the slip in the woods and somehow make it over the wall.

As he struggled through the creepers and bushes Dunbar cursed his own weakness. Greed, that ancient vice of man, had ensnared him into a lurid web of murder and betrayal. Now, in this tangled wilderness, which plucked his clothes and tore at his skin, he was discovering the price of his folly.

The sounds of his pursuers grew nearer. Dunbar changed direction and plunged on through the jungle-like undergrowth. His breathing grew tighter and his limbs began to tire, but fear and the will to survive forced him on.

Then without waning he broke into a small clearing. He paused and listened. The hunt was falling behind. He gulped for air. Suddenly he became conscious of another, different sound—a low rasping hiss—like a pit full of rattle-snakes about to attack. In front of him the vegetation began to move. He backed away with a scream of fear. The Krynoid, now ten feet high and sprouting suckers and tentacles, detached itself from the surrounding bushes and advanced toward him. Panic-stricken,

Dunbar pumped bullets into the towering mass of green, but they had no effect. It continued its relentless advance. Dunbar turned to run. As he did so he tripped in the dark over a hidden root and crashed to the ground. High above him the foul, hissing monster let out a blood-curdling screech and plunged downward for the kill!

9

Siege

The Doctor and Sarah stopped in their tracks as several shots rang out. Then a ghastly scream filled the woods. The sound came from no more than a hundred yards away and the doctor immediately set off toward it, tearing through the undergrowth at breakneck speed. Sarah stumbled after him.

Within a matter of seconds they were in the clearing. In the pale moonlight the Doctor made out a human body, barely recognizable, lying on the ground. Hovering above it, in full view, was the Krynoid.

The Doctor gripped his sword more tightly as the monster rose from its victim with a terrifying hiss and turned to face him.

"Doctor!" screamed Sarah as she rushed to his side. He quickly pushed her behind him for safety. Then the Krynoid let out a triumphant roar and started toward them.

It had advanced half way across the clearing when machine-gun fire suddenly broke out all around. The Doctor and Sarah threw themselves to the ground. The Krynoid faltered as bullets tore into its fleshy green exterior.

"Run to the cottage!" yelled the Doctor, and he

and Sarah scrambled to their feet and dashed off.

Hearing the Doctor's command, Scorby ordered his men to follow, but one luckless guard was dragged off balance by a powerful snaking tentacle. With a scream he disappeared into the center of the writhing, fibrous mass.

"Block the window!" ordered the Doctor as the others tumbled into the cottage. Two of the guards dragged a table across the room while the Doctor barricaded the door with heavy furniture.

"How do you do it, Doctor?" leered Scorby. "You should be compost by now."

"We'll all be compost if we don't keep away from that Krynoid."

"Krynoid?" repeated Scorby in puzzlement. "Is that what that thing is?"

Sarah turned to face him for the first time. "Yes. And it used to be called Keeler," she said bitterly. "Remember your friend? Now do you see what we're up against?"

The color drained from Scorby's cheeks. "That's . . . Keeler?" he stuttered in disbelief.

Sarah nodded.

At that moment Scorby's walkie-talkie started to bleep, "Yeah?" he said, still sounding shaken.

"Scorby, what was all that firing?" The sharp, distorted voice of his master crackled through the room.

"It's the Krynoid, Mr. Chase, it's got us trapped in the cottage."

"You idiots! Listen to me—whatever happens it must not be harmed. Is that clear?"

Scorby gave the Doctor a hopeless glance. "But you don't understand. It's ten feet high and it's already killed Dunbar."

"I don't care who it kills," screamed the voice

hysterically. "People are replaceable, the Krynoid is unique. It must not be damaged in any way. That is an order!"

The Doctor grabbed the walkie-talkie. "Chase, try to understand one thing." He spoke firmly and with authority. "The Krynoid is an uncontrollable carnivore and it's getting bigger and more powerful by the minute . . ." The receiver went dead. ". . . Chase! . . . Chase! . . ." The Doctor thrust it angrily back to Scorby. "Arrogant fool!"

He strode to the window and peered out. He could see nothing, but the sinister alien rattle was clearly audible to everyone in the room.

"Just how big is this Krynoid thing going to get?" said Scorby, panic creeping into his voice.

"Oh, about the size of St. Paul's Cathedral," replied the Doctor cheerfully. "Then it will reproduce itself a thousandfold and eventually dominate your entire planet."

Scorby's jaws dropped open and for once he was speechless.

The Doctor had moved away from the window during this exchange but now whirled around at the sound of splintering glass. The table blocking the window was hurled aside and a long green tentacle, about the diameter of a man's leg, snaked into the room. Pandemonium ensued as one of the guards started firing blindly. The tentacle thrashed from side to side knocking people and furniture in all directions. Then, catching hold of Sarah by the waist, it dragged her screaming toward the open window. Reacting quickly, the Doctor snatched up the sword and plunged it deep into the green protuberance. Its grip on Sarah slackened momentarily and the Doctor pulled her free. Then, as suddenly as it had entered, the tentacle withdrew.

"It can't get into the cottage," explained the Doctor, gasping from his exertions, "not for the moment at least. It's grown too big."

He peered out again through the smashed window. The low, menacing rattle could still be heard. Everyone in the room was trembling from the shock of the attack, and looking to the Doctor for the next move. Cupping his hands around his mouth he leant out into the darkness and called, "Stalemate for the present, Keeler. Can you hear me? Stalemate."

There was a deathly hush and then the air was filled with a strange, hollow, rusty voice. "The human . . . was . . . Keeler . . . now of us . . . now belongs . . ."

The Doctor glanced at the anxious faces behind him in the room. "I see. What do you want?"

"You, Doctor . . . You are . . . important . . ."

"How kind. Thank you."

"You have alien knowledge . . . You must be the first . . ."

Sarah took hold of the Doctor's arm. "The first?"

"I think it means I've been singled out for special attention, Sarah."

"Scorby!" cried the booming voice, like a giant tannoy system surrounding the cottage, ". . . Give the Doctor to us . . . your lives will then be spared."

Scorby raised his machine gun. "Sounds a fair deal to me, Doctor. How about it?" He took a threatening pace forward.

The Doctor stood his ground. "If you kill me, Scorby, you're finished. Nobody else has any idea how to fight that creature."

"I haven't heard any ideas from you so far,"

snarled Scorby. His machine gun was still pointing at the Doctor's chest.

"Unless the Doctor gives himself up . . . you will all perish . . . You have two minutes . . ."

All eyes in the room were trained on the Doctor. Sarah began to feel a prickly heat climb the back of her neck.

"Well?" Scorby slipped the safety catch.

"Fire!" said the Doctor abruptly. "Fire is the only thing that might affect it." He started to hunt among the debris, ignoring the gun still trained on his back.

"There's nothing here," growled Scorby suspiciously.

"Oh yes, there is," said the Doctor triumphantly, "a spirit stove." He blew the dust off it and unscrewed the top. "You're going to make us a Molotov cocktail, Scorby, and lob it from the upstairs window when I give the word. This will distract the Krynoid long enough for me to slip out. Then with a bit of luck the Krynoid will follow me and the rest of you will retreat to the safety of the main house. Quite simple, really." He beamed a smile around the room.

Scorby looked unimpressed. "It had better work, Doctor." He began to empty the kerosene from the stove into an old milk bottle.

"Where are you going, Doctor?" whispered Sarah anxiously.

"Out—if I'm lucky. The worst part will be trying to convince some flat-headed Army type that the world is being threatend by an overgrown mangel-wurzel." He turned away from the others in the room and lowered his voice. "I'll have to risk leaving you behind, Sarah."

Sarah nodded. It was more important now for

the Doctor to organize a proper resistance to the Krynoid while there was still a chance of stopping it.

Scorby finished the makeshift incendiary bomb and climbed the stairs. The Doctor cleared the furniture from behind the main door and eased it open a fraction. The hoarse rattling of the Krynoid was drawing closer.

"Right *now*!" yelled the Doctor and, yanking the door open, he hurtled out. Simultaneously there was a loud explosion and a sheet of flame lit up the interior of the cottage.

Running hard, the Doctor headed away from the cottage and into the dense black jungle. Behind him the Krynoid let out a bellow of pain and turned in pursuit. It was now at least twenty feet tall and, although possessing no limbs as such, its speed over the ground was astonishing. It slithered and glided through the trees like an advancing avalanche, smashing all before it.

As he plunged through the creepers the Doctor hoped his sense of direction had not deserted him. He was banking on finding the limousine which he and Sarah had abandoned many hours earlier.

Suddenly he was clear of the woods and standing on a gravel drive. With a gasp of relief he caught sight of the car still parked where he had left it. He bounded toward it and jumped into the driving seat. He could hear the trees crashing and toppling behind him and, above that, the angry roar of the Krynoid itself. Frantically he turned the key in the ignition. It wouldn't catch. Just as the roaring and hissing seemed almost on top of him the engine spluttered into life. Wrestling with the steering wheel, the Doctor spun the large car around and accelerated away.

As he did so, he caught the Krynoid in the full glare of the headlights. Its massive green trunk throbbed and pulsated, and the long clawing tentacles waved wildly in the air. In the split second it was discernible, this repulsive vision of unearthly terror burned itself into the Doctor's mind, never to be forgotten.

Then it was gone, and he was speeding through the cold black night in a race against time.

As the Doctor made his dash for freedom, Sarah and the others slipped quickly from the cottage toward the safety of the main house. Once inside, Scorby posted guards and lookouts and led Sarah to the laboratory. The room was deserted except for Hargreaves, looking slightly bewildered.

"Where's Mr. Chase?"

"He went out. To try and get some photos, sir."

Sarah registered surprise but Scorby, who was used to his master's bizarre ways, seemed unperturbed.

"All right, Hargreaves," he nodded. "Now listen . . . get some timber from the workshop. We've got to barricade all these ground-floor windows. Understand?"

"If you say so, sir." The butler departed on his errand.

Sarah glanced uneasily toward the window. "He must have got away." She tried to sound hopeful.

Scorby scowled darkly. "He's no fool, your friend. He got out and we're still trapped."

Stung by this remark, Sarah sprang to the Doctor's defense. He's only gone to get help. Somebody had to do it."

"Sure," came the sarcastic reply.

Sarah looked away. She felt very unsafe with this

repressed psychopath. Better to keep quiet and avoid provocation. She sank into a chair and began the long wait for the Doctor's return.

Outside in the grounds Chase was moving cautiously through the undergrowth. He was still wearing an immaculate pinstripe suit, and around his neck hung an expensive-looking camera.

To the ordinary observer he might have appeared crankish, almost comical, but to those few who knew him his madness was not a ridiculous aberration but a deadly, all-consuming passion—a love of plant life above all other life forms, including human. Chase was physically repelled by people. He reduced contact with them to the bare minimum; hence the black gloves to avoid touching them, and the elaborate safety precautions surrounding the house to stop them getting in. Apart from his immediate entourage he was a recluse, known only by name to the outside world. But within the high walls of his own domain Chase had created a different world—a luxuriant, peaceful world of green—a world in which, for moments at least, he could pretend to shed his human guise and commune with his beloved plants.

It was such communion he now sought with the Krynoid, this strange and wonderful intruder from another planet. He, Chase, would divine its true intent and impart this knowledge to the rest of mankind.

He pressed on gently through the foliage. Suddenly there it stood, a towering fibrous mass of green, swaying slowly from side to side in the moonlight. As Chase approached, it seemed to sense his presence, and from beneath the wrinkled folds of its bark-like skin a glistening tendril snaked out toward him, menacingly.

"No! No! Not me," cried Chase. "I want to help. I want to help."

The tendril wrapped itself around Chase and, lifting him bodily into the air, drew him in toward the cavernous folds of skin. Prodding suckers explored his body and face and he began to feel strangely drowsy. Then, just as he was on the point of suffocation, Chase found himself deposited once more on the wet grass. He lay there several minutes, gasping for breath. When he recovered the Krynoid had gone. He looked around, a weird, unnatural glint in his eyes.

"Yes, yes," he whispered. "The plants must win. It will be a new world . . . silent and beautiful."

He rose to his feet and like a sleepwalker moved slowly away in the direction of the house.

10

The Plants Attack

It was just dawn when the Doctor brought the large limousine to a screeching halt outside the World Ecology Bureau. He leapt out and ran up the steps into the tall building. Behind, a posse of wailing police sirens indicated that his mad dash had not gone unnoticed.

Sir Colin was arguing with a spruce-looking army major when the Doctor burst in upon them like a whirlwind.

"Doctor!" gasped Sir Colin, completely taken aback.

"Where's the brigadier?"

"Geneva," answered the major. "I'm deputizing. Major Beresford." He bowed stiffly.

"What's going on down there, Doctor?" asked Sir Colin, gathering his wits.

"Revolution is going on. The Krynoid is growing larger and more powerful by the minute. What's more, if my guess is correct, all the rest of the vegetation on this planet will shortly turn hostile as well."

A secretary entered and handed Sir Colin a piece of paper. As he read it he turned pale.

"This seems to confirm your theory, Doctor." He

real aloud. "A gardener, an agricultural worker and a young woman have all been found strangled by plants within a mile of Chase's estate." He looked up in dismay.

"The Krynoid is controlling them," said the Doctor, his expression darkening.

The major shook his head. "I don't believe it."

"I suggest you start believing it, Mayor," snapped the Doctor. "We're wasting time. I want you to organize flame-throwers, anti-tank guns and as many men as you can muster. Now!"

The major jumped into action as if bitten by a dog.

"I'm going back straightaway–and I need some argicultural spray defoliant. I'll give you two minutes, Sir Colin. Get it down to the car."

Sir Colin's office immediately became a hive of activity as the Doctor's orders were put into effect. Meanwhile, the Doctor picked up a phone and dialed a number he had memorized.

The phone rang loudly in the laboratory, startling Sarah who had been sitting alone. Gingerly she picked up the receiver.

"Doctor!" Her face lit up. "How did you . . . ?"

Interrupting her, he quickly explained what was happening, Sarah nodded, making mental notes as the Doctor issued instructions. Then suddenly they were cut off.

"Hello? Hello? Doctor?" Sarah jiggled the receiver up and down but the line seemed quite dead, as if the wires had been suddenly ripped out by someone. Or something. Behind her a pane of glass cracked like a pistol shot. She spun around, dropping the phone in alarm. The window, which five minutes earlier had been clear, was now obscurred by a mass of creepers. As she looked, the glass broke and the creepers inched their way into the room.

"What's happening?" cried Scorby from the doorway. He threw down a pile of timber.

"It must be the Krynoid. It's controlling the creepers!"

Another pane burst.

"Quick, help me board the windows," shouted Scorby, and he began nailing the planks across.

As the two of them struggled to fight back the creepers, Hargreaves raced in. "All the guards have gone!" he cried. "I think they've made a run for it."

"Just like a bunch of women," growled Scorby.

"I also heard a scream from the West Gardens," added Hargreaves. "I didn't go out."

Sarah looked concerned. "We'd better investigate." She started to leave.

"No. Stay put," ordered Scorby. "We can't risk it with that thing roaming about out there."

Sarah scoffed. "What was that you just said about women?" She ran from the room. Scorby hesitated, told Hargreaves to carry on boarding the windows, then followed Sarah out.

It was first light. Sarah's breath hung in the air as she made her way down the side of the house. Behind her she could hear Scorby's heavy footsteps on the grass. This time her own example had forced him to comply, but clearly when things got worse Scorby would be interested in saving only one skin—his own.

They were now nearing the thick undergrowth and had to pick their way carefully. Suddenly Sarah stopped. Sticking out of the long grass a few yards ahead was a human hand. Gingerly, she approached the body. A thick clump of trailing vines had wound itself tightly around one of the guards and strangled him to death.

"It's not possible," whispered Sarah, looking around in horror. The vine creepers were swaying eerily from side to side although there was no breeze.

All at once a twig snapped underfoot. Startled, Scorby and Sarah whirled around. Chase was standing in the bushes a few feet away.

"I obtained some fascinating photographs," he said. There was an odd, faraway look in his eyes.

Scorby ran to his side and shook his arm. "Mr. Chase, we're in desperate trouble. The plants are taking over!"

"Why not? It's their world. We animals are simply parasites after all." Chase smiled strangely. "I must get these developed." He turned on his heel and hurried off toward the house.

Scorby shook his head. "He's really gone."

"He's been gone for years if you ask me," replied Sarah quietly.

They retraced their steps to the laboratory. Hargreaves had successfully blocked up the remaining windows. Chase's eamera lay on the bench.

"Where is he?" said Scorby.

Hargreaves motioned toward the large ornate doors which led to the greenhouse. "Talking to his plants. I wouldn't disturb him if I . . ."

Scorby pushed the butler roughly to one side and threw open the doors. "Chase!"

At the far end of the cat-walk, almost hidden by the dense foliage, was the immobile figure of his master. He was seated crosslegged, in the familiar Lotus position of an oriental mystic, eyes closed, hands pressed together beneath his chin. His lips were moving rapidly as if repeating a litany but no words could be heard because the room was filled with a piercing electronic sound.

Scorby crossed to the synthesizer and switched it off. Oblivious, Chase continued his incantation.

"We shall have perfection . . . the world will be as it should have been from the beginning . . . a paradise of green . . ."

Scorby ran down the cat-walk and grabbed hold of the mumbling figure. "Chase, listen to me!"

". . . a harmony of root, stem, leaf and flower . . ."

"*Chase!*"

"It's no good," said Sarah. "He's in some sort of trance."

Scorby ignored her and continued to bellow at the inert form. "Chase, you've got to understand. We're going to be trapped here unless we do something. Your precious plants are starting to kill people."

Chase opened his eyes and gazed scornfully at the pleading figure before him. "The time has come. Animals have held sway on this planet for millions of years. Now it is our turn."

"What do you mean, your turn? You're one of us, Chase."

"No he's not," said Sarah. "Not any more."

Scorby turned to Hargreaves. "Come on. We've got to lock him up." He started to grab Chase under the arms. The butler hesitated, his sense of loyalty uppermost.

Suddenly Sarah let out a shriek. "Scorby! The plants! They're moving!"

As they looked the foliage on either side of the cat-walk began to close in, cutting off their escape to the door. A creeper wrapped itself around Sarah's ankle. Desperately she jerked herself free. Another caught her arms. Scorby and Hargreaves also began to struggle. A sinister shrill rustling sound began to build up in the room, as if the plants themselves were emitting a battle-cry.

Someone began to choke. "Help! Help!"

"Don't resist us. You have to die. All plant eaters must die." Chase's hollow voice rang in Sarah's ears but now it seemed far, far away. The blood pounded in her temples, her muscles began to tire, she couldn't breathe, she was being slowly throttled to death!

11

Trapped!

"Sarah!"

Through a green haze she saw the blurred outline of the Doctor and felt a fine spray of liquid on her face. Around her the seething vegetation began to fall away. A second figure, dressed in khaki, swam into her vision, making for Scorby and the butler. The room was filled with a terrible keening wail, as if the plants were dying.

"Stop it! Stop it!" Chase's mad voice shrieked above the noise.

The Doctor reached Sarah and dragged her to her feet. Scorby too was free but the butler had disappeared beneath the writhing mass of leaves.

"Animal fiends! You'll pay for this!" Chase struggled desperately past them and ran from the room.

"Quick, get out," ordered the Doctor, covering their exit with a jet of defoliant. The swirling mass of branches and creepers continued to harry them, but not so strongly, and they gained the safety of the laboratory.

The Doctor banged the doors shut and hauled a heavy filing cabinet into position to secure them. The creepers were already poking through the gaps in the door.

"I feel like I've been pulled through a hedge backward," said Sarah, smiling weakly.

"What is that stuff?" asked Scorby, catching his breath for the first time.

"The latest military defoliant. Still on the secret list. Sergeant Henderson helped me scrounge a few cans from Sir Colin."

"Nice to see you, Sergeant," said Sarah, "but are you all they could spare?"

"There's a unit on the way," answered the sergeant with a smile.

"Yes, and before they arrive we must clear the house of all plants," barked the Doctor. "They are the eyes and ears of the Krynoid." He started to tear out the experimental trays containing plants and seedlings, and the others quickly followed suit.

Within minutes they had successfully disposed of a hundred or so plants into an outside courtyard.

"That's all we can find for the moment, Doctor," said Sarah.

"Good. Back inside, everybody."

As they turned to re-enter the house a loud roar reached their ears and the stone walls of the courtyard began to vibrate. For a moment it seemed the house itself was about to fall down.

Sarah looked up and there, towering above the rooftops, was the Krynoid. It had grown to about sixty feet, and hundreds more tentacles protruded from its trunk-like body, each one capable of smashing a man to pulp.

"The door!" yelled the Doctor and he leapt to open it. I wouldn't budge. Someone had locked it from the inside!

"Chase!" exclaimed the Doctor and hammered on the door. But it was solid Elizabethan oak. They were trapped.

"Look!" screamed Sarah.

The Krynoid had moved closer and one of its giant tentacles was poised to swoop down on them. This time there was no escape!

Suddenly, there was a blinding red flash and the Krynoid let out a screech of pain.

"It's the major," cried Sergeant Henderson. "They're attacking it with the laser."

They watched transfixed as bolts of red lightning slammed into the upper part of the monster. Distracted by this new threat, the Krynoid turned from the courtyard and, letting out a deafening rattle, bore down on the small knot of soldiers operating the laser.

The Doctor saw the opportunity. "Quick! Follow me." He led the others at a gallop out of the courtyard and along the side of the house.

In the distance Beresford's commands rang out. "Ready—fire! And another—fire!"

The Krynoid was advancing steadily despite the laser and, deciding discretion was the better part of valor, the major ordered his men to retreat. As the khaki-clad figures scurried into the woodland, the Krynoid gave a final roar of defiance and turned its attention once more toward the house.

The major's diversion had created precious seconds for the fleeing group to find another entrance, and they were now heading back to the comparative safety of the laboratory.

"Well, at least the major had a go," said Sarah ruefully as they entered. "Even if it was like using a peashooter on an elephant."

Scorby, shaken by their narrow escape, sank into a corner. "I never thought Chase was so far round the twist," he muttered.

"Maybe he counted on the Krynoid sparing him if he sacrificed us," said Sarah.

The Doctor shook his head. "No. We were mistaken about who—or what—Chase is."

The others stared at him.

"You said he went out in the grounds with a camera and came back unharmed. I should have realized. He locked that door behind us because he is acting as a plant. He's in league with the Krynoid."

"Doctor, the radio's been smashed." The sergeant pointed to the broken apparatus which once kept Chase in contact with his patrolling guards.

"Now we're completely cut off," whispered Sarah. Behind the doors leading to the greenhouse the trapped plants could be heard clawing and scratching on the polished metal.

"We've got to find Chase," snapped the Doctor, "before he does any more damage." He strode out into the corridor. "Sarah and I will take this wing . . . you and Scorby check along there, Sergeant."

The two couples set off in opposite directions along the dim passageway.

Sir Colin Thackeray, looking sleepless and tense in the early morning light, paced impatiently up and down the gravel drive by the gatehouse. The main house was invisible from where he stood and nothing had been heard of Major Beresford and his men after the initial burst of firing. Behind Sir Colin, anxious and expectant, a second unit stood ready for action.

Then, appearing at first in ones and twos, Beresford's troops began to emerge from the woods. Breathing hard the major reported.

"We had to pull back. The laser was hopeless against it."

"And you haven't made contact with the Doctor?"

"Not yet. He must be trapped inside the house. I'm going to try and sneak through with a couple of men." He hurried off.

Sir Colin twirled his umbrella and pulled hard on the brim of his bowler hat. The Doctor was the only person with any idea of how to combat this alien menace. Somehow they had to get through to him.

Inside the house the Doctor and Sarah had covered the East Wing without coming across Chase. Now they linked up again with Scorby.

"No sign of him anywhere," said Scorby. The Doctor scrutinized his dark, sullen features. There was no telling whether he could be trusted—even in this desperate situation.

The sergeant ran up. "Doctor, there's a load of creeper breaking through into the corridor back there."

"All right, we'd better retreat to the lab." The Doctor led them smartly away.

As they disappeared, the lurking figure of Chase stepped from behind a pillar and glided off into the gloom like an evil ghost.

Back in the laboratory, the Doctor set about mending the two-way radio. Scorby crossed to the window and peered through a chink in the boards.

"It's like being under siege," he murmured nervously.

"Yes," the Doctor replied calmly. "Soon the Krynoid will be large enough to crush the whole house. We haven't much time."

As he spoke one of the wooden planks was forced away from the window, making Scorby jump.

"I'll try and find some more timber," volunteered the sergeant and hurried out.

"Be careful," Sarah shouted after him.

The sergeant made his way to the rear of the house where there was more likelihood of finding some spare wood. Too late he realized he was unarmed, he had left his rifle in the lab. He decided to press on regardless.

Suddenly he thought he heard a noise. He stopped and peered ahead. The passage was deserted. Then, without warning, a figure sprang from the shadows and struck him hard on the back of the head with a heavy metal spanner. Mercifully, that was the last the sergeant knew.

Quickly his assailant dragged the unconscious body through a doorway, and moments later re-emerged, smiling malevolently. He closed the heavy door and vanished silently into the shadows. Within seconds a strange, muffled noise penetrated the door, like a heavy machine whirling into action, or a hungry monster devouring its prey.

"Any hope, Doctor?" Sarah peered anxiously at the tangle of wires.

"Chase didn't do any irreparable damage. I've nearly fixed it."

"Well done, Doctor," sneered Scorby. He was huddled on the floor like a man who had given up all hope. "Why are you bothering? It's obvious your army friends have run away. We're as dead as mutton."

"Stop feeling sorry for yourself, Scorby," said the Doctor, eyeing him distastefully.

Suddenly, the whole room gave a lurch, the radio shot out of the Doctor's hands and large pieces of masonry fell from the ceiling, smothering them all in a choking white dust.

"This looks like the final attack," whispered the Doctor.

Scorby, sweating with fear, glanced toward the door.

"Don't be a fool, Scorby," said the Doctor, guessing his intention. "Everything that grows in the grounds is your enemy. You'll never make it."

But Scorby's nerve had snapped. He scrambled to his feet and tore out before anyone could stop him.

Gripped with panic Scorby reached the East Wing and hunted for a door that would let him out. The Krynoid could not possibly be on this side of the house. All he had to do was make it to the wall.

He found a door and pushed it open. With a shock he ran headlong into a mass of creepers but somehow clawed a way through. Once out in the open he set off toward the heavy undergrowth which lay between himself and the main road. As he ran, he snatched a backward glance at the house and gasped in horror. The whole West Wing, where the Doctor and Sarah were still trapped, was covered by the sprawling shape of the Krynoid, now over a hundred feet high. Its major limbs and tentacles had encompassed the roof and walls, like a giant spider sitting on its prey, and it was now beginning to slowly crush the solid masonry inward. At the same time the surrounding vegetation had grown larger and wilder and was covering the house at the points the Krynoid could not reach, blocking every window and exit.

Scorby had just time to take all this in before he plunged headlong into the murderous jungle which still separated him from safety. Tendrils and branches flapped menacingly as he drove his way through. He was not far from the cottage and the stream that ran near by. Once across that he would be almost at the outer wall. Cursing and swearing he stumbled into the shallow water and struck out for the far bank. Fifteen . . . ten . . . five yards . . . he was nearly there. Then, from nowhere, he felt a tangle of weeds wrap around his legs beneath the water. They were pulling him down! He lunged and thrashed about but the weeds were now around his body, trapping his arms, dragging him down, down, down beneath the icy water . . .

With a final swirl the waters closed over Scorby's head and he disappeared below the surface. The writhing weeds subsided, their deadly purpose accomplished.

"Hello! Hello!"

The Doctor fiddled desperately with the radio tuner but all he got was an unfriendly crackle. He shood his head angrily, dislodging bits of plaster from his thick locks. "Where's the sergeant? I need the major's wavelength."

Sarah looked up uneasily. The sergeant had been gone a suspiciously long time. "I'll go and find him," she said bravely. Before the Doctor could stop her she vanished down the corridor.

She had seen the sergeant take the corrdior toward the rear of the house, and she followed the same route. Besides the continuous rattle of the Krynoid outside she could now hear another sound, a knocking from inside the large hot water conduits which ran all around the building and provided special heating for the plants. Here and there holes must have appeared in the pipes for small bursts of steam shot out periodically. She guessed the whole system must be overheating.

With a flicker of fear Sarah realized she was nearing the crusher room. There was something lying on the stone floor ahead. It was the sergeant's green beret.

"Sergeant?"

There was no response. The door to the crusher room stood open. Sarah crept up and peered in. The room was empty, the giant machine at rest. She stepped inside.

"Sergeant?"

A movement behind her made Sarah spin around. Leering at her, a heavy spanner raised high to strike, was the evil figure of Harrison Chase.

12

The Final Assault

"The sergeant is no longer with us."

"Chase!"

"He's in the garden. He's part *of* the garden."

Sarah cast a glance of horror toward the crusher.

"We're both serving the plant world, the sergeant and I—in a different ways, of course. I have joined a life-form I have always admired for its beauty, colors, sensitivity. I have the Krynoid to thank for that, as it thanks me for its opportunity to exist and burgeon here on Earth. Soon the Krynoids will dominate everywhere . . . your foul, animal species will disappear!"

"And you will all flower happily ever after."

Chase's black-gloved hand gripped the spanner more tightly. "You and your kind are merely parasites, dependent upon us for the air you breathe and the food you eat!" His voice grew hysterical. "We have no need of you . . ." He began to advance on her. Sarah cowered against the wall, raising her arms to ward off the blow she knew was coming. Then, in a state of pure frenzy, Chase leapt toward her.

* * *

The Doctor was inwardly cursing himself for letting Sarah go off alone as he twiddled with the tuner. Suddenly, the crackling gave way to a voice.

"This is Scorpio Section. I say again this is Scorpio Section. Are you receiving me? Over."

It was the major.

"Hello, Beresford. This is the Doctor. What action are you taking against the Krynoid? Over."

"Hello, Doctor. The laser had no effect, but I managed to get nearer with a couple of men. The Krynoid is completely covering the house and beginning to crush it. All exits are blocked. I repeat, all exits are blocked."

The Doctor gripped the microphone tightly. "Listen, Beresford, by my reckoning you have less than fifteen minutes before the Krynoid reaches the point of primary germination."

There was a pause at the other end. Then a new voice came on the line. "Doctor . . . Thackeray here. What do you mean, primary germination?"

"I mean the Krynoid is about to eject its spores—thousands of embryo pods like the ones we found in the ice. The whole Western hemisphere will be inundated with them."

The Doctor heard Thackeray catch his breath. "How can we stop it?"

"There's only one way now, Sir Colin. A low-level attack by aircraft with high explosives."

"That will destroy the house too. What about you and the others?"

"Never mind us. Order that attack!" He switched off the receiver and headed for the door, his face a grim mask.

As he reached the doorway he paused and uttered a name softly beneath his breath, "Sarah." He had just signed a death warrant for the two of them.

Bound hand and foot, Sarah's inert form lay unconscious in the belly of the crushing machine.

"Three minutes. Go quietly, Miss Smith," uttered Chase with a sadistic grin as he pulled the starter lever.

The giant machine shuddered into life. The gleaming steel rollers gathered speed and began to descend toward Sarah's defenseless body. As the crescendo of noise built up Sarah slowly stirred and opened her eyes. A spasm of inexpressible terror shot through her entire being. She was powerless to move or even scream. From the wall, Chase observed her without emotion.

Suddenly the door was flung open and the Doctor burst into the room. With a yell of fury Chase leapt at him with the spanner. Expertly the Doctor parried the blow and thrust Chase backward into a pile of rubbishbins. Then, switching off the machine, he dived into it and lifted Sarah bodily to safety. As he did so Chase restarted the machine and hurled himself on the Doctor's back like a fiend possessed. The two men grappled precariously in the belly fo the machine, inches away from the whirling blades.

"Switch it off, Sarah!" shouted the Doctor. Sarah tried to reach the lever but with her hands tied she could not stop it. The rollers spun faster and nearer. Finally, by sheer muscle power, the Doctor managed to lift himself clear and drop over the side to the floor. He tried to haul Chase after him, but the madman had caught hold of the Doctor's arm in a vice-like grip and was pulling him back. He seemed to possess the strength of ten men and the

Doctor felt himself being drawn once again toward the grinding, chomping blades.

All at once, Chase let out a piercing yell and his iron grip slackened. His feet were trapped in the rollers and he was being sucked into the gaping maw of the crusher. Frantically the Doctor tried to pull him free but the monstrous machine would not disgorge its victim and suddenly, with a hideous scream, Chase was gone.

Shaking from his ordeal the Doctor staggered over to Sarah. "I tried to save him," he said. Sarah nodded mutely. Chase undoubtedly deserved to die, but it was not a death she would have wished on anyone. In a matter of seconds the Doctor had freed her and they left without a backward glance.

High in the sky a tight formation of Phantom jets streaked across the south of England, heading for Chase's mansion. A curt, matter-of-fact voice crackled in Beresford's earphones.

"We'll be with you in three minutes, Scorpio Section. Over."

"Roger Red Leader. Out." Beresford clicked off his receiver and crossed to Sir Colin who was staring thoughtfully at the ground.

"The planes are on their way."

"Is there nothing we can do to get them out?" Sir Colin's face wore a tortured expression.

Beresford shook his head sadly. "Nothing. Nothing at all."

"What are we going to do?"

Sarah was trying to keep up with the Doctor as he raced along the corridor. At every turn they were having to dodge falling masonry and crumbling walls as the Krynoid increased its strangle-hold on the house. Its echoing roar grew louder.

"We're going to fight our way out, Sarah," said the Doctor through clenched teeth, "but we've only got about two minutes in which to do it."

They were now at the rear of the building, where the Doctor had first entered, and he let out a grunt of satisfaction as they came upon the door. Gingerly he eased it open. A thick wall of vegetation completely blocked the exit and began to press forward into the corridor even as they stood there. The Doctor slammed the door shut and put his back against it. Sarah looked toward him in despair.

Suddenly the Doctor's eyes lit up. She followed his gaze. Several feet away was a door marked "Boiler Room," and leading out of the wall in all directions were the large central-heating pipes Sarah had noticed earlier.

"Steam! Highly pressurized steam!" exclaimed the Doctor and he wrenched open the door. Inside was a bewildering collection of knobs and dials and, jutting out from the floor, the top of the boiler itself. Steam was spurting from it in little jets and the whole system seemed about to explode.

The Doctor grabbed one of the boiling hot pipes with his bare hands and prised it free of its connecting valve.

"Open the door when I tell you, Sarah . . . and stand back!"

The Doctor gave another tug and the pipe tore away. Immediately a jet of superheated steam shot out of the end. "*Now!*"

As Sarah yanked open the door the Doctor carefully aimed the hissing, scalding jet at the thick tangle of creepers in the doorway. With a curious shrieking noise they began to wither and fall away.

"Follow me, Sarah!" yelled the Doctor and, flinging the pipe to one side, he plunged headlong into the foliage.

Overhead, the Phantoms screamed past on a low-level run. "Hello, Scorpio Section. We see your target. We're coming in to attack now. Over."

Beresford gave a last glance at Sir Colin who nodded imperceptibly. "Understood. Out."

The Phantoms banked and turned. "OK. Here we go, chaps. Let's turn it into chop suey!"

They started their run in.

Head down and arms flailing, the Doctor hacked a path through the deadly jungle. The entire vegetation of Chase's estate seemed to have closed in on the house and every yard was an effort. The trees and plants seemed alive—snatching at their arms and tripping their legs—so that they bobbed about like corks in a sea of green. Exhausted and breathless, Sarah began to weaken and the Doctor had to haul her bodily through the murderous tangle. Overhead, the whine of the approaching jets rang in his ears. He redoubled his pace.

Just as the plants seemed about to overwhelm them they broke through into a clearing. Ahead, the Doctor spied a pile of sawn logs. With one last effort he dragged Sarah to safety behind them. Across the tops of the trees he could now see the Krynoid dwarfing the house, its massive tentacles reaching to the ground.

As he watched, the first of the jets streaked in overhead and loosed its rockets into the side of the building. There was a blinding flash and a huge explosion which devastated one entire wing of the house, but the Krynoid still remained, its tentacles waving furiously above the chimney tops.

A second Phantom screamed into the attack, then a third and fourth. The Doctor and Sarah were hurled on their faces by the force of the explosions which rocked the ground and uprooted whole sections of woodland around them. Through the thunderous noise the Doctor suddenly heard the elephantine death-rattle of the Krynoid itself. The bombs must have hit it! A terrible, gigantic screeching filled the air then the noise ceased and everything went deathly quiet. The Doctor tapped Sarah's shoulder. Together they peered over the top of the logs. Chase's house, only a moment before enveloped by the mighty Krynoid, had vanished. The Krynoid too had disappeared and where they had both stood there was now only a smoking heap of ruins. The alien menace had finally been vanquished.

The Doctor and Sarah were seated comfortably in Sir Colin Thackeray's office, examining a battered roll of film.

"We found it in Chase's camera," explained Sir Colin. "The photographs are priceless now of course."

"It's a wonder anything survived that inferno," said Sarah, a note of sadness in her voice. The Doctor too looked rather glum, as if the strain of the last few hours had not yet passed from his mind.

"Well, Doctor," said Sir Colin, trying to sound cheerful, "do you think we've heard the last of the Krynoid?"

There was an awkward silence, then a faint smile appeared on the Time Lord's face. "Hard to say, Sir Colin. You see, the Intergalactic Flora Society—of which I'm the honorary President—finds the Krynoid a difficult species to study. Their researchers tend to disappear."

"I can imagine," chipped in Sarah. "A case of one veg and no meat."

Sir Colin chuckled. "Very neat, Miss Smith. By the way, speaking of societies, Doctor, the Royal Horticultural have got wind of this affair. They'd rather like you to address one of their meetings."

"When's this?"

"They suggested the fifteenth."

The Doctor took out his five hundred year diary and consulted it carefully. "Sorry. Out of the question. The next couple of centuries are fully booked. Anytime after that." He snapped the diary shut.

Sir Colin gaped at him. "I never know when you're serious, Doctor . . ."

"Send someone to talk to them about South American begonias. Much more the Royal Society's cup of nectar." He rose hurriedly. "Come along, Sarah."

"Where are we going?"

"Cassiopeia."

"Where?"

"A nice little spot for a holiday. It's time we had a break. Goodbye, Sir Colin." Before she could argue further the Doctor gathered up his hat and scarf and strode out of the room.

Sarah turned to Sir Colin. "Would you fancy a tiny excursion as well?" Her eyes twinkled with humor.

Sir Colin smiled back. "I'd be delighted—but my wife's expecting me home for tea."

"Sarah!" the Doctor's voice bellowed from the corridor.

"I'd better go," she whispered, "he gets a bit

tetchy now and then. It's his age, you know. Goodbye, Sir Colin." Sarah gave a little wave and ran out of the room.

Sir Colin crossed to the window and looked out with a certain sense of relief. His attention was caught by an old-fashioned blue police box standing in the car park below. He was sure he had never seen it there before.

As he watched, the Doctor and Sarah emerged from the building and walked into the box. The light on top began to flash, a strange wheezing and groaning sound reached his ears and the police box vanished into thin air!

Sir Colin blinked, shook his head as if he had seen a ghost, and decided he was in need of a good, long sleep.

SPECIAL PREVIEW

"What we always knew about Sherlock Holmes when he supposedly fell to his death at the Reichenbach Falls, we now know about Solar Pons—he is not dead; he has just been hiding."

—*St. Louis Post-Dispatch*

THE ADVENTURES OF SOLAR PONS

by
Basil Copper

based on the characters
and series created by
August Derleth

Come, once again, to Number 7B Praed Street, where Solar Pons, the master of deduction, awaits your arrival. Slouched in the cozy cavern of his armchair, his keen eyes fixed on the door, Solar Pons puffs thoughtfully on his pipe, pondering the strange and soul-chilling cases he has selected for your mystification.

Over forty years ago, when August Derleth inherited the mantle of Sir Arthur Conan Doyle, he created in Solar Pons a detective whose genius cannot be matched—perhaps not even by Sherlock Holmes himself! Now the pen has passed into the hand of the noted British author, Basil Copper, whose superlative storytelling abilities will astound and delight faithful followers and mystery lovers alike.

Here is the brilliant Solar Pons at his very best . . . clutching at elusive clues as he briskly sets apace into the ominous alleyways of old London in chase of crime. If you've not yet joined us in the eternal hunt, you are about to discover a new joy in a tradition that, alas, may have been lost forever, were it not for the reappearance of the remarkably ingenious and incomparable Solar Pons, whose entrancing effect on dyed-in-the-wool aficionados of detection is, indeed, elementary. It is time now to begin. The game's afoot!

(*The following pages have been excerpted from* The Dossier of Solar Pons, *#8 in the series, in which Dr. Lyndon Parker, Pons's faithful companion, relates "The Adventure of the Ipi Idol."*) *

More than an hour had passed and the lights had long been extinguished. I eased my position in the chair and waved my hand to dispel the heavy waves of blue smoke from Pons's pipe.

"Patience, Parker," he said softly. "I fancy the time is at hand. If he is to strike it must be done soon because he knows we are on the ground."

We had only a bedside lamp burning in the room and all the time we had been here Pons had been alert, listening for every footfall in the corridor. Half a dozen times he had darted to the room door, opening it a crack, surveying the corridor outside and then returning to his seat. There were two wall sconces still burning in the passage outside, leaving long stretches of shadow, and I understood from Pons that it was Colonel d'Arcy's habit to leave lights on all night whenever he had house guests.

Twice had the surly figure of Vickers been seen by Pons passing along the corridor during that time, but Pons had only smiled at my fulminations and had bidden me to be patient. Now there had been a deep silence for some while though my companion assured me that lights still shone beneath some doors, including that of Colonel d'Arcy.

I had risen from my chair and was taking a turn about the room when Pons jumped swiftly to his feet, holding his finger to his lips. At almost the same instant a terrible scream reechoed throughout the house. It was a woman's voice, hoarse and resonant with terror and it seemed to come from next door. Pons had already flung open the door, revolver in hand.

"As quickly as you can, Parker. It is life and death!"

I was swiftly at his heels, revolver drawn, as Pons flung himself at the door of Colonel d'Arcy's room. He hurled it open without ceremony. I shall never forget the sight that greeted us. The room was lit only by one solitary bedside lamp which threw a subdued glow across the apartment.

The bed coverlets had been thrown back but our attention was riveted on the end of the bed where the figure of a beautiful girl crouched, a look of absolute terror on her chalk-white face. The body of Miss Claire Mortimer was rigid with shock and horror. She was clad only in a dressing gown and her dark hair was awry and falling across her face.

"There, Parker, there!" said Solar Pons, his iron grip at my wrist.

I wrenched my glance from the frozen figure of the girl up toward the pillow. At first I could see nothing, then, from the tumbled white sheets, flickered the greenish coils of a snake. Its tongue darted from its mouth and a sibilant hissing noise filled the chamber. My throat was dry and my hand unsteady, but Pons's voice brought me to myself.

"A green mamba, Parker. The most deadly snake in all Africa! Your shot, I think."

I raised my revolver, hardly conscious of what I was doing. Yet I was myself again, my nerves calmed by Pons's reassuring presence. He moved closer to the girl, inch by inch, his derringer at the ready.

The crack of my pistol, the acrid sting of powder and the flash were followed by a rain of feathers from the bed, and the bullet cut a vicious gouge in the planking of the floor beyond. Splinters flew in the air as the snake writhed for an instant and then was still.

"Well done, Parker!" said Pons, supporting the fainting girl and dragging her from the bed. I ran to his side and helped him move her to a chair.

"See to that thing, Parker. Make sure it is dead."

Perspiration was running down my cheeks, but my nerves were steady now as I cautiously approached the bed.

"My aim was true, Pons," I said, unable to keep the pride from my voice. Footsteps were sounding in the corridor now, and the room seemed full of people. I was only vaguely aware of Bradshaw, Tolliver, Mrs. Mortimer, and the dark visage of Vickers.

Light flooded the room from a ceiling fixture, and at the same instant I managed to cover the remains of the snake with the bedding. Pons shot me a glance of approval. The bearded face of Colonel d'Arcy appeared. He elbowed his way through without ceremony.

"Good God, Mr. Pons! Claire! What on earth has happened?"

"The lady has had a nightmare," said Pons gently. "All is well now. But I think it would be best if she spent the remainder of the night with her mother. And I should keep this room locked if I were you."

The colonel instantly grasped the situation.

"It is nothing, ladies and gentlemen. Would you please return to your rooms. I very much regret the disturbance."

The sobbing girl, soothed by her mother, was led from the room, and the remaining guests, with curious glances, shortly followed. Our host hurried away, leaving Pons and me alone in that suddenly sinister room.

"I don't understand, Pons," I said.

Solar Pons ran a finger along his jaw, which was grimly set.

"I am not entirely clear myself, Parker," he said. "But we shall no doubt learn more in a moment."

Indeed, our host returned almost at once and faced us somberly, locking the door behind him.

"I cannot thank you enough, gentlemen. If anything had happened to Claire . . . What was it?"

I pulled back the bedding. Colonel d'Arcy surveyed the mamba with sick loathing on his face. He clenched his fists and his features began to suffuse with blood.

"By God, Mr. Pons, we must discover the wicked mind behind this . . ."

"It is almost over, Colonel," said Pons quietly. "Though I do not know how Miss Mortimer came to be here."

"She complained of a draft in her room," said our host. "Mine was the more comfortable so I gave it to her. The fireplace has more heat, for one thing."

Pons nodded.

"Evidently, he could not have known that," he murmured. "I am afraid Parker and I have made a mess of your floor . . ."

Colonel d'Arcy stared at us in amazement. He came forward and wrung my hand, then turned to Pons.

"I am not an emotional man, gentlemen, but Miss Mortimer means more to me than anything in the world."

"I understand that, Colonel," said Pons, frowning down at the thing that still lay in bloody tatters on the bed. "But it will not stop here. Our man knows we are on him. The shot alone would have warned him. He will act quickly. We must act more quickly still."

Colonel d'Arcy looked bewildered.

"I am in your hands, Mr. Pons. What do you want me to do?"

"I think this evil man will strike again before the night is out. This time at you, Colonel. I want you to go to my room or Parker's and spend the night there. No one but the three of us must know of this."

"Anything you say, Mr. Pons. What do you intend to do?"

Pons went to stand by the fireplace, holding out his thin hands to the glowing embers. His lean, feral face had seldom looked more grim.

"First, I would like the disposition of the guests this evening and the exact location of their rooms."

"That is easily done," said the colonel.

Pons listened attentively as he gave us the information. He nodded with satisfaction.

"Ironic is it not, Parker?"

"I do not understand, Pons."

"No matter. You will in due time."

He turned briskly to the colonel.

"We must spend the rest of the night in your room, Colonel. I fancy a revolver or a stick will be adequate protection against the menace of the Ipi idol."

He looked at me, his eyes alight with excitement.

"Come, Parker. The game's afoot!"

London's most renowned detective since Sherlock Holmes

SOLAR PONS

by August Derleth

"A tour de force...avowedly an imitation... it is more, it is an excellent series in detection in its own right."
—Chicago Tribune

☐	40-634-7	Regarding Sherlock Holmes	#1	$1.95
☐	40-635-5	Chronicles of Solar Pons	#2	$1.95
☐	220543-3	Memoirs of Solar Pons	#3	$1.25
☐	230585-2	Casebook of Solar Pons	#4	$1.50
☐	220629-0	Reminiscences of Solar Pons	#5	$1.25
☐	40-636-3	Return of Solar Pons	#6	$1.95
☐	230870-8	Mr Fairlie's Final Journey	#7	$1.50
☐	40-267-8	Dossier of Solar Pons, by Basil Copper	#8	$1.95

PINNACLE-BOOK MAILING SERVICE
P.O. Box 690, New York, NY 10019

Please send me the books I have checked above. Enclosed is my check or money order for $________. (Please add 50¢ per order and 10¢ per book to cover postage and handling. New York State and California residents add applicable sales tax.)

Name____________________________________

Address__________________________________

City____________________State/Zip______________

Please allow approximately four weeks for delivery.